BOOK ONE OF **THE MISEWA SAGA**

THE BARREN GROUNDS

DAVID A. ROBERTSON

PUFFIN CANADA
an imprint of Penguin Random House Canada Young Readers,
a division of Penguin Random House of Canada Limited

First published in hardcover by Puffin Canada, 2020
Published in this edition, 2021

10

Manufactured in Canada

Library and Archives Canada Cataloguing in Publication

Title: The barren grounds / David A. Robertson.
Names: Robertson, David, 1977- author.
Series: Robertson, David, 1977- Misewa saga ; bk. 1.
Description: Series statement: Book one of the Misewa saga |
Previously published: Toronto : Puffin Canada, 2020.
Identifiers: Canadiana 20200407961 | ISBN 9780735266124 (softcover)
Classification: LCC PS8585.O32115 B37 2021 | DDC jC813/.6—dc23

Library of Congress Control Number: 2019955922

www.penguinrandomhouse.ca

Penguin
Random House
PUFFIN CANADA

For Emily, Cole, Anna, Lauren, and James

THE
NORTHERN
WOODS

THE
GREAT
TREE

BARREN GROUNDS

ᒥᓴᐧ
MISEWA

THE
SOUTHERN
WOODS

TREE
BRIDGE

CAMP

OCHEK'S
TRAPLINE

N

W   E

S

SWAMPY CREE GLOSSARY AND PRONUNCIATION GUIDE

SOUNDS:
É – ay
Í – ee
I – ih
A – ah
O – oh
E – eh

Amisk ah-misk: beaver
Api ah-pih: sit
Arikwachas eric-watch-ahs: squirrel
Askí ah-skee: earth, ground
Astum ah-stum: come
Awas ah-wahs: go away
Ehe eh-heh: yes
Ekosani eh-koh-sah-nih: thank you
Iskwésis ih-skway-sis: girl
Kayas kah-yas: long ago
Kihiw kih-ewe: eagle
Kisakíhitan kiss-aw-kee-hih-tuh-n: I love you
Kisémanitou kih-say-man-ih-too: Creator
Kiskisitotaso kih-skih-sih-toh-tah-so: don't forget
   about who you are

Mahihkan mah-hih-kahn: wolf

Misewa miss-ah-waa: all that is

Miskinahk miss-kih-nack: turtle

Mistapew miss-ta-pay-oh: big foot (giant)

Moshom moo-shum: grandfather

Muskwa muh-skwa: bear

Mwach mwa-ch: no

Napéw nah-pay-oo: man

Ochek oh-check: fisher

Ochekatchakosuk oh-check-at-chack-oh-suck: the fisher stars

Oho oh-ho: owl

Pimíhkán pih-mee-kaan: pemmican

Pinésisak pih-nay-sis-ack: birds

Pisiskiw pih-sis-koo: animal

Pisiskowak pih-sis-koh-wack: animals

Sisipak see-see-pack: ducks

Tahtakiw tah-ta-koo: sandhill crane

Tansi tan-sih: hello

Wapos wah-puss: rabbit

ONE

Morgan's head was pressed against her pillow. The alarm on her phone had just been snoozed again, and her plan to leave early for school was slipping away each time she reached forward with a groggy hand to silence the incessant beeping. Still, she refused to poke around the screen lower, where a simple touch would shut the alarm off permanently. She had good intentions to wake up, stay awake, and get out of bed.

The thing was, she was so darn comfortable.

A rhythmic, crunching sound replaced the alarm with this last strike of the snooze button, and a scene of a blizzard came into her mind. Morgan was walking through it, across a seemingly endless field. There was a square light in the distance, but she never got closer. When she tried to move faster, her body wouldn't allow it. She kept taking the same heavy steps that led nowhere, her feet crunching through the snow.

Morgan tried to imagine something else.

She should have been able to. It was not a dream. She knew she was awake. She pressed her eyelids shut so tightly that her entire face scrunched together like a raisin, to force something else into her mind, to force herself back to sleep and into an actual dream. But she couldn't get rid of the image, or the crunching.

Then it dawned on her: the crunching sound had been in time with her heartbeat. With her ear pressed against the pillow, her pulse announced itself forcefully and unrelentingly. All she had to do was lift her head. It was a cosmic design to get her out of bed.

Morgan kicked off her sheets like she was in a karate class, sat up, and the sound went away. She stayed like that for a minute, staring at the white walls, the blizzard stubbornly following her even now, until the alarm jolted her into movement. She silenced it again, then checked the time. Good. It was still early. Morgan set about the task of getting ready for school.

After all, this had been the plan all along.

Morgan's bedroom had a tall, narrow window that faced the street. Opposite the window, in the back corner just above the floor and beside the headboard, were two pipes protruding from the wall. They were cut down, capped off, and out of the way. She guessed that her bedroom used to be a bathroom, but in the two months she'd been here she had never bothered to ask, because the answer felt obvious.

Where else would you stick the oldest foster kid?

The room had thin carpeting that didn't quite match the hallway carpet, which made Morgan think that it had been purchased at a discount carpet store. She had hung clothing, mostly hoodies, on a series of hooks at the back of her door, and taped a modest collection of posters to the walls. Finally, there was a floating shelf for her books. Fantasy books mostly. Old ones, because Morgan liked how books used to be written. She liked the worlds that authors imagined and how she could imagine herself in them. She would read books on her bed, facing the window. She'd lie on her stomach, kick her feet in the air, and get lost. Other times, she would just sneak to the attic. There, she could really be alone, and she could really escape.

Escaping was the plan this morning, just not into another world. Rather, Morgan intended to get out of the house and on her way to school solo. It would be a peaceful walk on her own for once, without Eli, the new foster kid. Over the last week, since he'd arrived at the house, it felt like she'd become a glorified babysitter, even though, at twelve, Eli was only a year younger than her.

Morgan got dressed in ripped jeans, a white T-shirt, and a black hoodie, and tied her black hair into a loose ponytail. She pulled the door open in slow motion to prevent any squeaking from the hinges: success. Halfway there. Now there was just the matter of the hallway. She took one soft step, then another, all without even a whisper of a sound.

Morgan felt like a ninja.

To her left was Eli's bedroom. She could see the mound of his body underneath the *Star Wars* comforter their foster parents had bought him prior to his arrival. The only personal touch in the room and it wasn't even his. At least Morgan had her things on walls and hooks, and even clothes scattered on the floor. If Eli hadn't been sleeping in the bed right now, you'd never have known that somebody was living there. There was only Eli and the oversized drawing pad he brought everywhere, like Linus and his blanket.

More ninja steps followed.

The only thing that worried Morgan was Katie and James; their bedroom was directly adjacent to the stairwell, as though they'd known beforehand that they'd have to contend with a teenaged girl sneaking around. Luckily, the door to the stairwell was open. This meant all she needed to do was continue on her improbable run of silent steps. She could already picture herself walking to school alone. The sun would be shining, the grass emerald green, the birds chirping. There'd be no snowstorm, no square light in the distance that never got closer, no crunching footsteps.

She was almost home free. She put her foot down quietly. *If I* did *want to sneak out one night, I could totally do it,* Morgan thought. She'd run away before, which wasn't quite the same as sneaking out. Not from Katie and James's place, but from her last foster home. More than once. That was what had brought her here.

She took another step.

Creak.

Morgan stiffened. Maybe nobody would wake up. The peaceful, isolated walk to school could still happen, right? She wouldn't have to look back to ensure Eli was still with her, lugging that drawing pad with him. He was a small kid for his age, so the drawing pad looked comically big wedged between his arm and his torso. She wouldn't have to try to make conversation with him, because he hadn't said much since arriving here. She could just put her earbuds in and take her time.

"Morgan?" James asked from the bedroom. "Is that you?"

Morgan sighed. Why did James have to have super-human hearing?

"Yeah."

On the plus side, at least now she could go back to sleep for an hour.

When Morgan got up again, having, ironically, slept in, everybody was awake and breakfast was waiting for her. Arranged neatly on her plate, as though James was competing in a cooking show on the Food Network, were scrambled eggs, two strips of bacon, hash browns, and a perfectly quartered orange.

Morgan's stomach grumbled so loudly that everybody must have heard it: Katie, sitting across from her; James, sitting to her right, watching to see how Morgan would react to the food; and Eli, to her left, looking down at his own plate.

"Wait a minute." Morgan inspected the plate of food more thoroughly. The scrambled eggs resembled a mop of curly hair. The bacon strips were decidedly fat lips. Two orange slices were ears, and the final two were eyes.

James snorted, trying to stifle a laugh.

"Are you serious?" Morgan buried her face in her palms.

"Too bad he doesn't have a nose, because the food smells great," James said with a guffaw.

"You know I'm thirteen, not three, right?" Morgan asked. "I think you forgot about the, you know, one in front of the three or something."

"*James* thought it might . . ." Katie gave him a deliberate side-eye. "Cheer you up?"

"Cheer me up," Morgan echoed.

"You've been . . . you've looked upset since moving here, almost all the time," James said, glancing at Katie for approval. "I . . . *we* . . . just want you to feel at home here. Comfortable."

"But this isn't my home," Morgan said. "The last seven places weren't my home either. Do you think"—Morgan took a deep breath, a technique she'd learned to remain calm—"a breakfast made into a face is going to change any of that?"

"It's just what families do." Katie dabbed at her mouth now as though she wanted to wipe away the words she'd just blurted out. She tried again. "We're new to this, Morgan. This is our first family." She reached across the table and put her hand on James's. "It was always just us before you came."

"I thought the breakfast was an *egg*-cellent idea." James bit his lip.

"A pun? Seriously?" Morgan, although her stomach had been roaring, pushed the plate away and crossed her arms. She took more deep breaths. If she blew up, they'd want her gone; then it would be eight homes, not seven. As ridiculous as James was, as annoyingly earnest as Katie was, they weren't *awful*. Not the kind of awful she'd had before. Okay, her breakfast had been made into a face. It was better than finding a note on the kitchen table telling her to *"Eat what's left"* and sitting alone with a bowl of dry cereal because there was only expired milk in the fridge. Cereal from the bottom of the box, crumbs that only milk could save.

"Puns are what dads use," James said. "It's like their language. I was trying—"

Morgan saw Katie give James a short, subtle slap on the hand she'd been holding.

"You're *not* my dad!" Morgan said.

"We're trying, Morgan." Katie's voice was quiet, as though this might temper Morgan's outburst.

"And *you're* not my mom," Morgan said. At least she hadn't raised her voice. That was a considerable feat, because her blood was at boiling temperature. "Stop trying so hard, and just, I don't know, lay off."

"And do what? What do you want us to do?" James asked.

"I don't know. I'm the kid here!" Morgan stood up. That's when she noticed that Eli's meal, too, was shaped into a face. They had breakfast-face twins. "Really!?"

"Well, he hasn't been . . ."

"Why do you expect him to be just, like, happy? He got here last week! Let him be sad. He's going to be sad, okay?" Morgan, for the first time, felt a connection to Eli. "Come on, kid, we've got to get to school."

Eli had been sitting there quietly, unmoving, probably in shock. His brown, almond-shaped eyes were staring at the plate as if he, too, had just noticed the food face; his lips were pursed as though he wasn't going to utter a word, even if he'd wanted to say something; and his feet seemed glued to the floor until, at Morgan's urging, he got up from the table and came to stand beside her.

"Morgan . . ." Katie started.

"Sit down," James said. "Finish your breakfast at least. I know you're hungry."

"Do you want me to do something with your stupid breakfast?" With trembling fingers, Morgan took one of the slices of bacon, broke it in two, and positioned a piece over each eye. She made the other bacon slice into a frown, then pushed the plate towards James. "There! You've looked too happy lately; I'm just trying to help."

"That's not fair," James said.

"You know what's not fair?" Morgan asked. But she stopped, even though Katie and James seemed attentive, ready to hear what she had to say. Unlike the plate of food, they did not look angry. They looked concerned. The only person that Morgan's plate looked like was, well, Morgan. She shook her head. Her planned speech about moving families, houses, about not even remembering her real home (if she wanted to remember it at all) was abandoned. She just shook her head. "Never mind."

She grabbed Eli's hand and brought him with her towards the front door. They got their shoes and backpacks on, and Eli took his drawing pad. Morgan worked very hard not to slam the door, and didn't.

This was also a feat, but she took no pleasure in it.

TWO

It was early November in Winnipeg. The air was crisp, and each blade of grass was coated in frost. Morgan cut across the lawn. Eli followed. Her feet crunched against the ground, and it made her think of the blizzard all over again. She double-timed it to the sidewalk. Her breath escaped in puffs of smoke, which may as well have been coming out of her ears, but she couldn't tell whether she was mad at Katie and James or herself. She decided that it was a combination of the two. She let out a loud grunt.

"Why are you angry all the time?" Eli asked.

Morgan glared at him for a second, and Eli recoiled, as if he'd been punched in the stomach. They kept marching towards school. Truthfully, she was kind of surprised that he'd said anything at all. She'd not yet heard him string that many words together at one time.

She tried to distract herself from her anger by observing the neighborhood. The endless run of two-story houses, each almost identical to the one next to it. The too-perfectly manicured boulevards that were more like putting greens you'd find at a golf store. The absence of graffiti sprayed on walls. There were white picket fences, basketball hoops attached to garages—even some Christmas decorations. They passed a couple of people walking dogs (all some form of doodle—Labra or Golden). The people nodded and smiled at Morgan and Eli, but Morgan just looked away.

"Could you at least slow down?" Eli asked.

He was struggling to keep up. His drawing pad kept slipping from under his arm, and every time it did, it slowed him down further.

Morgan breathed out deliberately and waited for him to catch up. "I'm not angry all the time. I'm angry *now*."

"You're—"

"You can't just say that," Morgan continued, cutting him off. "You can't ask '*Why are you angry all the time?*' when I'm just angry *now*. That's like saying a clown's happy all the time when their smile is just, like, painted on."

"That doesn't make any sense," he said.

"Well, I'm not angry all the time, so hopefully *that* makes sense," she said.

"You're angry at home and when we walk to school and at school," he said.

"How would you know if I'm angry at school?"

"I've seen you at school and you look the same way you do now—you're just quieter about it."

Morgan crossed her arms and sped up. He could just walk faster with his stupid drawing pad. "Stop watching me at school. That's weird. Especially because you're in seventh grade and I'm in eighth grade. There are rules."

"What rules?" he asked.

"Just rules, that's all!"

Morgan watched Eli too, though. He sat in the corner of the gym during lunch—on the floor, even though tables were set up. Every lunch hour, separate from everybody, his drawing pad balanced perfectly on his lap, scribbling away at whatever he liked to draw. It wasn't fair that she'd told him to stop watching her, when she watched him. But she felt obligated to keep an eye on him, just as she usually felt obligated to walk him to school (except for trying to ditch him this morning). He'd been around for only a week, but she felt like she knew him better than that. He reminded her of herself, when she was younger. At a new house, before new houses became part of her life. The irony was that while Morgan watched Eli draw, sitting by himself in a corner of the gym, she'd be sitting by herself at a corner of a table.

"I'm not angry at school. I'm shy at school, okay?" she said. "There's a difference."

Eli shrugged. "Why are you shy at school, then?"

"Because I don't like talking to anybody and I don't think anybody likes talking to me. We have an unspoken agreement to avoid each other. Me and . . . everybody else."

"If you don't talk to anybody, then how do you know if they don't like talking to you?"

"I liked you better when *you* didn't talk," Morgan said. "Plus, you're not exactly a chatterbox at school yourself, or *anywhere* for that matter."

For a while they just kept walking.

"It's not just that people wouldn't like talking to me; I don't think they'd like me *period*," Morgan said, as though they'd been talking the whole time.

"*I* like you," Eli said.

Morgan stopped abruptly, forcing Eli to stop too. He almost dropped his drawing pad.

"You hardly even know me." Morgan reached forward and flicked his drawing pad with her index finger, gently. "Plus, you're always drawing in that thing, so how do you even have time to like me?"

Eli held out the drawing pad and flipped to a page. It was a picture of the lunchroom, in pencil, full of kids eating their lunches, and there was Morgan, off to the side, sitting on her own, looking at the ground.

"Oh," Morgan said. "Eli, wow."

Eli closed the pad.

Morgan kept walking. Eli followed.

"How've you been to so many homes?" he asked.

"I don't know," Morgan said. "Stuff happened."

"What kind of stuff?" he asked.

"I run away," she said, "or they don't like me. Or I run away *because* they don't like me. I get older and, you know, they want a cute Native kid. And I can tell, so, I don't know . . . I guess I act like a jerk. They're saviors, you know. Like, all of them. Katie and James too. They want to save kids like us."

"I like them," he said.

Morgan took a deep breath, then half smiled. "Yeah," she said under her breath. "I do too."

The sun rose steadily over the twenty-minute walk and melted the frost, making the boulevards and trees glitter.

The neighborhood looked pretty, but Morgan always felt detached from it—no matter how high the sun rose, no matter how many times she walked the same route, and whether Eli was trailing behind her or not. It was one of several routes Morgan had taken to one of several schools, coming from one of several homes, and it was hard to think of what was different from one placement to the other. The only constant was that they'd all been in the same city.

"This is your first home, right?" she asked.

Eli looked forward, as though the glittering blades of grass had caught his attention. As though he wasn't ignoring her.

Finally, he nodded.

"I don't remember much about my first," she said, "but I know what it felt like. Like I was empty, and even though the house was full, it felt empty too. Does that make sense? I was like, I don't know, three."

"I was home," he said. "*Home* home . . ." He shrugged. "And then I wasn't."

"How'd it happen?" she asked.

"I don't want to talk about that," he said.

The school was up ahead. A long, flat brick building set against the backdrop of a large field that, too, was shimmering in the early-morning sun.

"I was too young to remember," she said. "All I know is that my mom didn't want me."

"How do you know that?" he asked.

"How could she?"

As they got closer to the school, they were joined by a throng of students funneling into the wide concrete walk that led to the front doors. Morgan made herself thinner, avoiding both physical and eye contact.

A gust of wind shouldered its way through the mass of middle schoolers, and when it collided with Morgan and Eli, Eli's drawing pad went flying through the air. It danced in the wind until it landed on the street, where it was promptly run over by the 68 Grosvenor bus.

"No!" Eli cried.

Without looking, he turned to run after it. Morgan grabbed his backpack and pulled him out of the way of an oncoming car. His drawing pad was run over again in the process and the pages went flying.

"Are you trying to get killed or something?" Morgan said.

"Let me go!"

Morgan looked both ways, saw that traffic was clear, and followed him onto the street. They gathered the pages together and piled them into a messy, muddied stack of art. Eli slumped on the curb, and Morgan flipped through some of the pages. With the exception of that drawing of her, his illustrations were all of villages within beautiful land-scapes, with animals walking on two legs through forests or along canyons or over mountains. Some were of lands in the middle of summer, some were colored with the warmth of autumn, others were made to face the harsh bite of winter. They looked like places straight from the fantasy novels Morgan loved.

She sat next to Eli on the curb, put his drawings aside, and placed her arm around his shoulders.

"These are amazing," she said, "even though they aren't all of me."

Her humor fell flat.

"They're all ruined," Eli said.

"Where did you get the ideas from? Do you like reading fantasy?" she asked.

"They're stories from my community," he said.

"Sooooo . . ." She picked up the pile of art and placed it on her lap. "The art is ruined but the stories aren't?"

"I guess," he said.

"Could you draw them again?"

"I guess," he said again. "But that's . . ." He looked at his drawings resting on Morgan's lap, then looked away, as though he couldn't stand to see them in their condition. "My dad got me that pad before I was . . ."

"Oh. Sorry."

THREE

Morgan walked Eli to his locker as she'd done all week, fulfilling a promise she'd made to Katie and James. "Just make sure he's settled," Katie had instructed. He clearly wasn't "settled" now, though—he'd carried his ruined illustrations with his head drooped, the intricate, expert pencil lines soiled by tire tracks across the paper.

Eli's locker was at the far end of the school. Morgan had to pass by her own locker to get to his. It meant that she had to walk the distance of the school, all the way there and all the way back, navigating through swarms of grade sevens and eights pushing in one direction or the other. To avoid them, Morgan engaged in a sort of dance. She wondered if Eli noticed this. How weird did she look, contorting her body to get through the crowd like she was a jewel thief trying to avoid a thousand laser beams?

"Well, here you are." Morgan watched while Eli opened his locker and placed the drawings inside carefully, as if they were made of glass.

Eli hung his backpack on one of the hooks inside the locker, then pulled out a binder and textbook. Math. Morgan had English Language Arts first period.

"Alright, I'll see you at the front doors after school." Morgan moved to leave, then stopped and turned back. "Or at lunch." She winced immediately. He had nothing to draw on anymore. "I bet if you told Katie and James about what happened, they'd get you a new sketchbook, just like the one you had," she said quickly.

"Nothing could be like the one I had," he said.

"Okay, it won't be from family, but . . ." She trailed off. "All settled?"

Eli nodded. "Yeah, sure."

When Morgan got to her locker, it was 8:47 a.m. Her class was just across the hall, so with all the time in the world she stuck her head inside her locker like a middle-school ostrich. The more time she could spend there, the fewer students would be around when she crossed the hallway.

The contents of Morgan's locker consisted of a neat stack of binders and textbooks, a magnetized mirror on the inside of the door that she used to keep an eye on who was coming up behind her rather than to check for zits, a page-sized poster of her favorite band taped to the back of the locker, and her class schedule taped above that.

A few minutes passed before Morgan decided it was safe to move. She'd hung her backpack from a hook and had started to pull out the book and binder she needed for

ELA when she spotted someone approaching in the mirror. It was Emily Houldsworth. And instead of just walking past Morgan to get to their class, for some reason, Emily stopped. Morgan looked away from the mirror to avoid eye contact, because Emily was just standing there. Morgan hoped that Emily would move on, but she didn't.

"Good morning, Ghost," Emily said.

Morgan turned around in slow motion to face Emily. This was happening and there was nothing Morgan could do to avoid it. "Ghost?" Had the other kids given her a nickname?

Emily must have read her confusion. "I'm just used to giving people nicknames," she said, then provided a final, one-word explanation. "Hockey."

"Right." Morgan was left to figure out what "Ghost" meant, but it wasn't exactly a crazy riddle to solve.

Emily looked Morgan over, head to toe. "I love those pants."

Ripped jeans? Morgan thought. *What's to love?*

"They look like authentic rips," Emily said. "Not store-bought rips. That's an important distinction. Well played."

"Thanks?"

Morgan looked over Emily's wardrobe. She was a short white girl with the physique of a gymnast. She had wavy, dirty-blond hair tied back into a loose ponytail, an Ice Cube shirt that, Morgan was certain, was meant to be ironic, a pair of canvas sneakers, and black yoga pants. Morgan felt she should reciprocate, even if Emily didn't look as though she expected it, but she didn't know what to say. *Cool shirt*, Morgan thought, as if Emily could read her mind.

Morgan wasn't sure if Emily talked to her because they were locker neighbors or if Emily was actually just nice. When she dissected it, she thought it was likely the latter. Emily never sounded sarcastic or like talking to Morgan was something she'd been put up to. And the new nickname didn't seem malicious. Emily wore a spring jacket for a AAA hockey team, even when it was hot outside, and she'd said it like they were teammates, like Morgan might call Emily something like "Houldsy."

"Hey." Emily waved her hand in front of Morgan's face. "Earth to Ghost."

"Sorry," Morgan said.

"That's alright," Emily said. "It's like when I see you with one of your books. Totally in another world."

"It's not that I'm bored of you," Morgan blurted out. *Bored of you?* Morgan cringed. Was there a hole she could crawl into? Could she *actually* stuff her head into the locker? "I like your shirt?"

"Thanks. It's ironic," Emily said.

Morgan caught herself laughing. Emily locked surprised by it. For some reason, this made Morgan want to hide even more. She checked the time on her phone: 8:56 a.m.

"We should go sit down," Morgan said.

"Did you finish your poem?" Emily asked.

"Yeah." Instead of reading a book last night, she'd taken her pink Hilroy scribbler, dusted it off, literally, and worked on it for a few hours in the attic. In the exact spot she usually sat to read. The lights weren't installed up there yet, so she used a mix of moonlight and street light. "I kind of just threw four stanzas together."

"What? I worked on mine all week." They stopped at the classroom door. "I need to get an A."

"Don't you always get As?" Morgan asked.

Emily shrugged. "I don't get As, I don't play hockey. That's the rule."

Morgan put her hand on the doorknob. She could see through the window that the class was full and ready to start. Mrs. Edwards was at her desk, shuffling papers.

"Want to read mine?" Emily asked.

"Why?"

"I just really want to hear yours," Emily admitted. "Thought you'd offer. You read so much, you must be awesome at writing."

"Oh, I don't . . ." Morgan could feel the poem she'd written last night stuffed into her back pocket. She'd ripped it out of the Hilroy scribbler that morning and put it there. "Just because I read doesn't . . . I mean, I like to write, it's just that—"

"It's alright," Emily said. "Don't worry about it."

The classroom door swung open. Morgan had been leaning against it and stumbled inside. It made all the kids break out into laughter. Thankfully, Morgan didn't actually fall, but still, damage had been done.

Right then, she did want to be a ghost.

"We're about to start," Mrs. Edwards said.

The class settled. Emily walked in and announced to their teacher, "We were talking about the assignment."

Morgan sat at the front of the class beside the windows that overlooked the skating rink and River Heights Community Centre. With an empty desk behind her and to the right, she was out of the way. She took her seat and pretended that she couldn't feel kids still looking at her. She pretended they couldn't see her at all.

Good morning, Ghost.

Mrs. Edwards had platinum-blond hair that fell over her shoulders. She always overdressed for school. Today, she was wearing a shiny black sequined dress, as if ELA was a cocktail party. Her desk was populated by a cup full of pencils and pens, a framed picture of her husband and son, and ten books neatly arranged at the front, held in place by wooden lion bookends. All ten were copies of *Lyrics to a Song*, a poetry book that Mrs. Edwards had written.

The students lined up to hand in their poetry assignments, and Morgan intentionally went to the back of the line, so by the time she arrived at her teacher's desk, there was already a neat stack of poetry. She reached into her back pocket and pulled out the crumpled piece of paper.

"Sorry about that." Morgan cleared her throat.

Mrs. Edwards picked Morgan's poem up from the pile as if it was a piece of trash. "What's this?"

"My poem," Morgan said.

"I see." Mrs. Edwards slid the poem against the side of the desk repeatedly to try to flatten it, like it was a bill that a candy machine wouldn't accept.

"Do you think this is appropriate?" Mrs. Edwards asked.

"No," Morgan whispered.

"I want to know how much pride you think you have to have in your work, Morgan."

"I'm sorry, Mrs. Edwards. It won't happen again."

"You're happy with this?"

"Yes." It wasn't that she hadn't worked hard on the poem. It was just that she'd worked hard on it fast.

"Alright, Morgan." Mrs. Edwards sighed.

The students were left to watch the last part of a film they'd started the day before, *Finding Forrester*, because, Mrs. Edwards announced to her students, "I just can't wait to read these beautiful pieces." It was her favorite film, she'd said last class, because it was about writing and she could relate to it. William Forrester had only ever written one book, and so had she. "It's just the life of a writer," she'd explained. "Your work is never really done. Some writers get stuck wanting to do something perfect, and once they think they have, well, lightning doesn't strike twice."

Morgan wondered if Mrs. Edwards really thought that *Lyrics to a Song* fell into that category, but she had to credit her for even publishing a book in the first place.

Mrs. Edwards was efficient. Ten minutes before class ended, she handed back their poems with their grades marked in red.

Morgan received hers last.

It had no red ink on it whatsoever.

"See me after class," Mrs. Edwards whispered to Morgan with what looked to her like an apologetic smile.

"Why?" Morgan looked over her poem as though she might see a red letter somewhere, hidden in the folds of a crumple mark.

"Just do," she said.

When the bell rang and the classroom had emptied, Mrs. Edwards took Morgan's poem and read it silently. Morgan watched her eyes move back and forth. When she finished, she handed it back.

"Is it bad?" Morgan asked.

Mrs. Edwards looked up at Morgan and held her eyes for a moment before reciting, *"Have all the greatest words been said? Then nothing more to do but hush. No phrases honeyed sweet as daisies, nor lines to make the crimson rush."*

Morgan just sat there, hands crossed on top of the desk.

Mrs. Edwards cleared her throat. *"Have all the poems been written? Then nothing more to do but hide. No shields with rhymes as hard as steel—"*

"I know what it says," Morgan snapped, but caught her tone. "Sorry, Mrs. Edwards, it's just that . . . I know what it says and I thought it was good."

"What's it about, Morgan? What are you trying to say?"

"It's about . . . I don't know." Morgan searched for the right words. "Writing. It's about not being able to write because, like, everything good's been written already. It's got layers."

"Is that what you're passionate about?" Mrs. Edwards asked.

"I'm passionate about writing, sure," Morgan said.

"Technically, the poem's really well done," Mrs. Edwards said. "But, Morgan, writing is about heart, and I'm not feeling that here. You are *so* talented, I can see it, but you don't write with any heart."

"Are you calling me the Tin Man of poetry?" Morgan asked.

"Well, if you are, then I guess that makes me the Wizard of Oz," Mrs. Edwards said. "I know you're capable of better, and I'll grade your poem when you've tried again. That's my job as a teacher."

"This isn't fair." Morgan's chest felt hot. "Can't you just give me a B or something? A C+ even?"

"Hand something new in by tomorrow. Write from your heart, not your head, and I'll grade *that* for you," Mrs. Edwards said.

"I . . ." Morgan felt hot all over her body now. She was back at the dining room table, looking at food made into faces. She wanted to explode. But she heard Eli's voice, asking her why she was mad all the time. It sounded clear, like he was standing beside her. She closed her eyes, took a deep breath. "I'm *not* mad all the time."

"Pardon me?" Mrs. Edwards said.

"Nothing. Fine, I'll do it," Morgan whispered.

She stuffed the poem back into her pocket and left the room silently, as though she was moving in whispers too.

FOUR

L unch was Morgan's least favorite time of day. Surrounded by the entire student body, she felt most isolated. Kids sat in the same place every noon hour, in easily definable groups. Jocks, who divided into subgroups depending on their respective sport—basketball, hockey, volleyball, soccer. Kids who were destined to take advanced classes in high school. Skaters, who performed impossible tricks off the steps of the school until shooed away by whichever teacher caught them. There was a long list of cliques. Some kids crossed over. Some kids did not. But everybody seemed to have *somebody*.

Morgan sat in the same place each day just like everybody else, but she sat alone.

She'd bought fries today and was stabbing at them while watching Eli, the only other kid who was alone. He was wearing a Radiohead T-shirt and Army green cargo pants, with his hair in a tight braid. His shoulders were slumped, his head was slumped, his entire body was slumped, sitting on the floor. A plate of food he'd bought from the cafeteria was resting by his feet, untouched. She might have continued torturing her poor food but just then a cool hand touched her own. Morgan looked up to see Emily standing by her—it was the first time Emily had approached Morgan away from their lockers.

"Hey," Emily said.

"Hey," Morgan said uncertainly.

"Can I sit with you?" Emily asked.

"Uhhh." Morgan looked around at the table as though she had to make space for Emily. She didn't. "Sure."

Emily sat across from Morgan, placed her lunch bag on the table, and zipped it open. She pulled out a plastic container and opened it to reveal little containers of Caesar salad with chicken strips, a mandarin orange, and trail mix with sunflower seeds, pumpkin seeds, and raisins.

Morgan shoved a forkful of fries into her mouth.

"What did those fries ever do to you?" Emily asked.

Morgan swallowed. "Huh?"

"You're annihilating your fries." Emily reached over and picked up Morgan's plate for a moment to show her the state of her food. It wasn't pretty.

"Collateral damage," Morgan said.

Emily had been chewing a slice of orange and almost choked on it. She patted at her chest while staring at Morgan confusedly, her face turning red.

"You okay?" Morgan asked.

"Yeah." She caught her breath. "I just didn't know you were funny."

"It wasn't *that* funny," Morgan said, looking down at her plate of mashed fries.

"Seriously, Ghost." Emily poked Morgan's hand with her index finger to make Morgan look at her. "What's going on with you?"

"Why do you even want to sit here?" Morgan asked.

Earlier in the year, another kid, one of the skaters, had sat with her, acting all suspicious. He was talking to her, but glancing away, like, every second. Morgan noticed a table full of his buddies snickering, watching them. He'd been put up to it by them. She guessed there was something funny about sitting with the new Native kid.

"I float," Emily said. "I'm a floater." It was true, she was. She was one of the kids who could sit with several different cliques effortlessly. "I saw you sitting here looking kind of upset, kind of mad, serial murdering your fries, and thought, 'Hey, this seems like a good idea.' I guess I'm a risk-taker."

"I'm not going to stab you with my plastic fork, don't worry," Morgan said.

"See? You *are* funny," Emily said.

Morgan smiled, but when she caught herself smiling, she stopped, like it was a dirty secret she didn't want out.

"So," Emily said, "what're you mad about? What's up?"

"It's about the poetry assignment," Morgan said. "Mrs. Edwards didn't give me a mark because I can do better, according to her. I have to redo it. By *tomorrow.*"

"Well, at least you didn't fail, right?" Emily said. "That doesn't sound like a defense for french-fry homicide. Just . . . write a better poem?"

"She said I have no heart, pretty much," Morgan said. "And I wanted to, like, scream at her. Tell her that her poetry book is lame, or something like that."

"But you didn't, right?" Emily asked.

"No, but . . ." Morgan stabbed another fry. "I always have this hot feeling in my chest, and you know when you've done something wrong and you feel so bad about what you did that you can't even say sorry about it?"

"Okay, I'm confused," Emily said. "You didn't, right?"

"It wouldn't have been the first time I blew up at somebody today," Morgan said, "if I had."

"So . . . you shouted at somebody, wanted to shout at somebody else, and now you're beating yourself up about it?"

"I *think* I need to reset the karmic balance of my life somehow."

Her eyes rested on Eli again. In her mind, she flipped through all the pictures he'd drawn. He must have made some of them right where he was now. And while Eli had said that she always looked angry at school, he always looked content while drawing. Like her books, his art was an escape. Without it, no doubt he had to think about being away from home, being in this strange school, being in a strange house with an angry, jerk-face girl.

Emily poked Morgan. "Hey, I'm still here, you know."

"We've got Art next period, right?" Morgan asked.

"Yeah. Why?"

"Because it's about time I did something nice today."

A few minutes into Art class, with Mrs. Bignell demonstrating how oil painting was done, Morgan felt something hit the side of her arm. She decided to ignore the projectile, whatever it was. A spitball. A paper ball. Any kind of ball. She kept her eyes forward and tried to be interested in how Mrs. Bignell was painting the petals of a flower. *I bet Eli totally kicks butt in this class*, Morgan thought. She stopped paying attention to the teacher, and her impressive lilac, and took inventory of the room. There had to be a drawing pad somewhere, one that was comparable to Eli's.

Another object hit her arm.

"Stop it!" Morgan hissed at whoever was throwing things at her.

"Is everything okay, Morgan?" Mrs. Bignell asked without turning her attention away from her lilac.

"Yeah, sorry," Morgan said.

"You'll paint a beautiful lilac, then, won't you?" Mrs. Bignell asked.

"Yes, Mrs. Bignell."

"Perfect." Mrs. Bignell put the finishing touches on the petal she was painting and moved on to the next one. It was very likely that the kids would not get an opportunity to paint their own flowers today.

Morgan looked for what had been thrown at her; two neatly folded pieces of white paper were scattered by her shoes. She looked around the class to see who could have thrown them, and her eyes met Emily's. When Emily nodded towards the papers, Morgan picked them up and opened them.

The first one read: *Hey, what's the plan? What do you have to do that's nice?*

Text me. 204-555-3474. That was the second one.

Mrs. Bignell was still going strong. Morgan slid her phone out of her pocket and texted Emily the following message: Kid living with me ruined drawing pad. Getting him a new one.

Morgan sent the message, and it made a *swoosh* sound. She quickly put her phone on silent and closed her eyes, like she was two, like it would make her invisible. It didn't. When she opened her eyes, Mrs. Bignell was standing over her. She did not look impressed.

"Sit outside of class until it's over," Mrs. Bignell said.

The class all said, "Oooooooh."

"Mrs. Bignell, please. I won't make another sound, I promise."

"Sorry, Morgan. You've disrupted the class twice already. You're done."

I kept the class awake! Morgan imagined saying to her teacher, heat simmering in her chest. But instead, she left class deflated.

In the hallway, she slammed her back against a locker and slid to the floor.

Moments later, she received a text.

Emily: Plan B?
Morgan: Don't have one.
Emily: Kid living with you . . . First Nations, braids?
Morgan: Yeah.
Emily: How much do you want a drawing pad?
Morgan: Doesn't matter anymore.

Morgan waited for Emily to respond. She saw the three dots in the gray circle, which meant that Emily was writing something. The three dots seemed to be there for a long time. Finally, Emily texted: What kind of drawing pad?

Morgan perked up. She wrote: Really?

Emily: Class could use more excitement.
Morgan: THANK YOU. One of the big ones.
Emily: On it.

Morgan waited. There were forty-five minutes left in class, and she wished that she'd brought a book with her to kill the time. Instead, she imagined how Emily would steal the drawing pad. It became a fantasy adventure heist. The class was full of snow, like the scene in her head that morning. Their classmates turned into rabid animals. Emily had to fight her way through them to get to the drawing pad, which was being guarded by the fiercest wolf of them all: the Bignell Wolf. No matter. Emily was armored with hockey equipment and a hockey stick with a blade that was an actual blade. Emily fought her way through the animals, then faced down the Bignell Wolf in an epic confrontation, eventually knocking it into the pit of despair where, if legends were true, the wolf would slowly disintegrate over thousands of years in a pool of watercolors. Emily stood triumphantly with the drawing pad raised over her head.

The bell rang.

Morgan jerked to attention, thrust out of her daydream. She watched the line of students filtering out of class, waiting for Emily. It felt like an eternity until she appeared, carrying a large drawing pad.

Morgan shot into a standing position. "You got it!?"

"I got it," Emily said.

"How?"

Morgan ran through the whole adventure sequence again. No, of course it hadn't been like that. But it could have been no less exciting. A heist, all done under the cover of silence. Emily had undoubtedly managed to steal the drawing pad, get back to her desk, and conceal it (that seemed most impressive, since it was huge), all without alerting Mrs. Bignell.

"I asked her if I could have it, and she said I could," Emily said.

Morgan's brow furrowed. "What?"

Emily repeated what she'd said, word for word, but slower.

"And that's it? She just . . . gave it to you?"

"She just gave it to me." Emily snapped her fingers. "Like that."

"Oh."

"Anyway"—Emily handed Morgan the drawing pad— "here's the thing you wanted for the sake of karma and all that."

It was the same size as the pad Eli's father had given him, just not the same brand. Morgan flipped through the pages, checking to see if there were already drawings on the white pages.

"It's perfect, really. Sorry if I'm being weird. I was . . . daydreaming."

"About a drawing pad?"

"Something like that."

They started off towards their next class, the last class of the day, which was Math.

"So, just to be clear," Emily said, "the drawing pad is for, and I quote"—she took out her phone and read the text Morgan had sent her—"'the kid living with me." By *me* I mean *you*."

"Eli," Morgan said. "That's his name."

"Is he your brother?" Emily asked. "Because that's cold if he is. Calling him 'the kid living with me' and all that."

"No, he's not my brother," Morgan said. "He's a foster kid."

"Really? Did your mom get a foster kid that looked like you?" Emily asked. "Feel free not to answer if that's a stupid question. Actually, it's for sure a stupid question."

All Morgan really heard was *mom*, and everything else after that kind of blurred together. "I don't have a mom."

Emily cupped her mouth. "Oh my god, I'm so sorry. Your mom's—"

"No. She's not dead. At least, I don't think she is. I—" Morgan closed her eyes. "I don't care if she even is. I just don't have a mom, not since I was a baby. I'm a foster kid too."

"I'm sorry."

"Don't be," Morgan said. "I'm not. And this . . ." She held up the drawing pad in a desperate attempt to change the subject. "This is awesome."

"I have my moments. And you can take all the credit."

"Thanks."

Morgan still wasn't sure how Eli would react. It wasn't the drawing pad his father had given him, so would he even want it? But the drawing pad wasn't his father. Losing the drawing pad didn't mean he'd lost his father any more than losing his drawings meant that the stories he'd drawn stopped existing. Either way, she'd tried. And so much of it was thanks to Emily. Getting the drawing pad was Morgan's idea, but Emily was the one who had actually got it.

"Why . . ." Morgan thought for a moment longer, figuring out how to ask what she wanted to ask. "Why are you being so nice to me?"

Emily didn't think long about her response. She tilted her head, scrunched her eyebrows together, and asked, "Why wouldn't I be?"

The bell rang.

Math had always been hard for Morgan, especially algebra, which they were studying now. But Emily's response felt like a more complicated problem to solve. Still, Emily had sounded so matter-of-fact. Why *wouldn't* she be nice to Morgan? She'd asked it rhetorically, as though the answer was obvious.

What's there about me for anybody to like? What do I even like about myself? Morgan thought. It felt like the world's hardest algebra question, and by the time class was over, she'd settled on the fact that Emily being nice to her was more a reflection on Emily than it was on her.

Eli was waiting for Morgan at the bottom of the steps out front of the school, just as he always did at the end of the day. She broke off from the swarm of kids and stopped at the top of the stairs with the drawing pad hidden behind her back, ready to surprise him. He was sitting hunched over, just like in the lunchroom. Morgan took the steps all the way down to the sidewalk, then turned to face Eli.

"Hey," Morgan said.

"Hey," Eli said.

"How was your day?"

"Fine."

"I was thinking, when we're home you might want to draw in my secret hiding place."

"I don't have anything to draw on, remember?" He had yet to look up.

Morgan took the drawing pad out from behind her back. "You could draw, and I could read, or work on my stupid poem, I guess. You'd like it up there. It's quiet."

"I said . . ." Eli looked up and saw the drawing pad.

"Here." She handed it to him.

He opened it, flipped through the pages as she had. It was as if he could already see all the drawings he was going to draw, all the fantastic stories that he'd created in his old pad. "You got this for me?"

"Yeah," she said. "I got it for you."

Eli stared at the drawing pad for quite a long time, then looked at her. "Why would you do that?"

Morgan tilted her head, scrunched her eyebrows together, and asked, "Why wouldn't I?"

FIVE

organ and Eli got home in record time, thanks in large part to Eli, who was walking faster than Morgan had ever seen. They didn't talk much. He couldn't wait to use the drawing pad, she could tell. As he walked, he checked every few seconds to make sure it was still snugly under his arm. He hadn't even asked Morgan where her secret hiding place was, and for a kid not to ask about a secret hiding place, well, his mind had to be somewhere else.

It wasn't really a secret hiding place. It was more like a forbidden place, and even that made it sound more exotic than it really was. The attic was on the third floor of the house. There was a flight of stairs that went halfway from the second floor to a landing, followed by another flight of stairs that took you the rest of the way.

"Here's the thing," Morgan said when they got home. "My secret hiding place is the attic, and it's really just that we're not allowed up there. Has James had that talk with you? The 'dos and don'ts'?"

Eli shook his head. "Not yet."

"He probably doesn't want to scare you off," she said. "In short: the attic's getting renovated into a family room or something, and because there's, like, a hazard everywhere you step, we're not allowed up there."

"What kind of hazards?" he asked.

"Never mind that." She brushed it off. "It's kind of like a curfew, you know? To be safe, you're supposed to come home before eight o'clock at night, but what's really going to happen if you come home at nine? There aren't *hazards*, really."

There actually were, but Morgan was of the opinion that, once Eli was up there, he'd see that the benefits outweighed the risks. So what if there were nails on the ground and exposed wires? They were *dead* wires, so, whatever.

"So . . . it's just an attic," Eli stated.

James was a doctor, Katie a teacher, and neither of them got home until around five o'clock, often later, so Morgan knew she had plenty of time to show Eli what she meant. She started to lead him up the stairs.

"Eli, you draw all those pictures with super pretty locations and walking animals and it's all so magical and amazing and yet . . ." She stopped for a moment, with one more flight of stairs to go. "And *yet*, you think an attic is just an attic?"

Eli shrugged.

They kept going, and soon were in the attic, looking out over its grandeur.

"*So it's just an attic,*" she said, repeating Eli's words and shaking her head. She gave him a nudge. "Come on."

Morgan suspected that the large open room used to be two bedrooms. She'd arrived at the house with the attic in mid-construction, and two months later, it was still in mid-construction. As far as she could remember, the construction guys had been there only twice. If they hadn't left their tool bags and some other equipment behind, you would never have guessed that they were doing work at all, or that they even existed.

It was the skeleton of a room. There was plywood flooring throughout, mostly deconstructed walls with the electrical wires that had been cut off from their power source exposed, and scattered piles of debris waiting to be taken away—sections of drywall, cut-up pieces of plywood, light fixtures, nails and screws and wire and broken glass.

The only *slightly* curious thing about the attic, other than to imagine what the room might look like in a billion years when it was finally finished, was a painted-over door on the wall beside the stairs that, at one point, might have been a closet when the attic had bedrooms. There was definitely space behind the door for there to be *something*—it didn't open to the outside of the house or anything like that—but really, Morgan had no idea what that something could be. There were layers upon layers of paint. You couldn't even see where the door ended and the doorframe began. And it didn't seem like the renovation plans included any work on the door and whatever lay behind it.

"So, where do you read and write and stuff?" Eli asked.

"Ah!" Morgan raised her index finger. "I was hoping you'd ask that. Follow me, little one."

"Hey." Eli's face scrunched up like he'd stuck a lemon in his mouth.

"Sorry! You're not little; I was just being dramatic."

"I *am* little, but you're making me feel weird about it."

Morgan led Eli to the window that looked out over the street. The window also, to this point, had been left mostly untouched. Only its frame had been stripped away. On the floor in front of the window there was a Morgan-shaped space cleared of any debris.

"There's no electricity so I use the flashlight on my cell, or the streetlight when my cell dies," Morgan explained.

There was a book leaning against the wall under the window. Morgan picked it up, then lay down on her stomach exactly where she had lain down each night she'd come up here, safe from any hazard. She opened her book to the page she'd dog-eared and started reading. Every few lines, she looked to the side to check on Eli, who just stood there at first, looking out the window. But then he started to kick away debris to make a space for himself, and eventually he sat down beside Morgan. He flipped the drawing pad to its first page, opened his pencil case, and took out a pencil.

Morgan smiled.

She liked that this was no longer a place just for her—it was for both of them. She didn't remember much about the first foster home she'd been taken to, only that she'd felt very alone. Everything was so big and she was so small. This was Eli's first foster home, and though he was much older than she had been, she could tell that he felt kind of the same thing. Alone. Now maybe he wouldn't feel that way. Not so much at least.

After that, Morgan gave most of her attention to her book, and she could tell that Eli was giving his attention to the empty page in front of him, full of possibilities. For a good while, the only sound was the flip of a page. Morgan figured that Eli was taking his time, thinking of the perfect thing to draw for his first work of art in the new book. She bet that he felt the same excitement she felt on the first page of a novel.

The prospect of a new world.

Finally, out of the corner of her eye, she saw his pencil hit the blank white page, as white as the blizzard she'd pictured first thing that morning. As soon as it did, loose strands of hair swayed in front of her face.

She blew them off to the side and kept reading.

Moments later, her hair was in her face again. This time, she had felt a subtle breath, cool against her skin.

"Would you stop that?" she asked.

"Stop what?"

"Blowing on me, obviously."

"I wasn't blowing on you," he said. "I'm just sketching something."

Morgan peeked over at Eli's drawing and immediately forgot everything. It looked like he was creating some kind of figure. Not a human, but something that walked on two legs.

"What are you drawing?" she asked.

Eli stared at it as though he hadn't just drawn it. "I don't know," he said. "I'm kind of just making it up, I guess."

"Cool." She nodded her head, impressed. Even just the start of it was awesome, the few pencil strokes he'd made to create the humanoid animal. It looked just as good as anything in the other drawing pad, the one involved in the hit-and-run. One last look, and she went back to reading.

She got a lot more reading done when she was up there alone, she realized. *But I* for sure *am earning some good karma*, she thought.

She hadn't gotten more than a line into reading when, again, cool air rushed against her cheek, this time stronger than before.

"Okay!" Morgan slapped her book shut and slammed it against the floor. A cloud of dust erupted from the plywood and danced in the darkening light. "I was cool with it; now I'm not."

Eli dropped his pencil as if it were burning his skin.

"I'm just *this* close"—Morgan pinched her index finger-tip perilously close to her thumb—"to revoking your secret room privileges, Eli, I swear."

"I felt that," he whispered.

"*Yeah.*" Morgan pushed herself up into a sitting position and threw her arms into the air. "No kidding. You're blowing on me and it's creepy!"

"I'm not blowing on you," Eli said, his voice trance-like.

"You're not blowing on me," Morgan stated. "Then what's blowing on me? It came from your general direction. The attic isn't haunted."

"My paper did it."

Morgan stared at Eli, and the room was dead quiet until she burst into laughter. Eli, however, was not laughing at all.

"Eli, your paper did it?" She could barely get the words out.

"I'm not lying."

The more Eli sat there, staring at Morgan stone-faced, the less she felt like laughing.

She caught her breath.

"There's probably a draft or something," she said. "It, like, went across your paper, hit me in the face . . . I swear, though, if you're doing it, *don't*."

"It *came* from my paper," he said deliberately.

Something about the way he said it made her reconsider his claim, even though it was just about the most ridiculous thing she'd ever heard. More ridiculous than her daydream about Emily stealing Eli's drawing pad.

"Okay," she said. "Do it again."

Eli hesitated. He reached for the pencil a few times before finally picking it up. He let the tip of it hover over the paper, ready to draw. The pencil was a millimeter from the white surface when Morgan heard the successive beeps that always rang out when the front door opened.

"Kids!" Katie called, all the way from the first floor. "Come down for dinner! I got takeout!"

Eli pulled the pencil away from his drawing and slipped it back inside its case.

"To be continued," Morgan said.

SIX

Takeout? Not one time, since Morgan had arrived at the house, had Katie and James gotten takeout.

Morgan and Eli left behind the mystery of the windy drawing pad—it had probably been a draft anyway; Eli must have been mistaken—and scrambled to get out of the attic so as not to get caught there. (James had never explained what the consequence would be, but Morgan didn't want to find out.) By the time they got down to the first floor, James was home too. He and Katie were standing together in the kitchen, waiting. James was usually easy to read, but the expression he wore now was hard to describe and equally hard to interpret. He had a genuine smile, but at the same time, it looked like he was constipated. Morgan's best guess was excitement and nervousness rolled up into one. But why?

"I'm kind of freaked out right now," Morgan admitted.

Eli said nothing.

"We're allowed to do something special for supper, aren't we?" Katie asked.

Morgan sniffed the air. Takeout usually had a distinctive smell, depending on where it was from. Everybody knew when they were passing McDonald's, for example. McDonald's had a smell. But this one . . . she couldn't place it. Morgan caught Eli sniffing too. She looked at him for an answer, but he just shrugged.

"Special why?" Morgan asked.

"You'll see!" Katie said.

"Is this because of breakfast?" she asked.

"No," James said, and he appeared to be stifling laughter at the memory. "But we do"—he looked at Katie—"have to talk about that."

"Later," Katie said.

"Yeah," James said. "It's just . . . it was dumb of me to make faces out of the food, but I don't think it was appropriate for you to act the way you did. We wouldn't reward you for that."

"Fine," Morgan said, and she decided that she may as well collect more good karma. "Well, I shouldn't have made a mad face out of your food, so I'm sorry."

"Thank you, Morgan," Katie said.

"Alright," James said, nodding. "Apology accepted. And I'm sorry for treating you like a kid. There will be no more faces made out of food."

"We're learning." Katie looked at Morgan, meeting her eyes, and then at Eli. "We've never had foster children before. We've never had children before. If you just let us try . . ." Katie's eyes started to glisten, but she gathered herself. "Why don't we go eat?"

What was up with that? No house that Morgan had been to previously had had somebody like Katie or James. No foster parent had looked close to tears, in a good way, because of her presence. Mostly, they'd seemed to want to help, even if their attempts had been misguided. As Morgan had told Eli, Katie and James were trying to be saviors for the poor Native kids. There were some, though, who were just trying to collect some extra money by taking in a foster child. There was one house Morgan had been in, when she was nine and ten, where she was treated fine, she guessed, but every time the family (they had their own kids too) went out together, like for a movie or something, they left Morgan at home in front of the television. They didn't even want to spend ten dollars on her for a movie ticket. They'd never intended for her to actually be family.

She'd always thought that Katie and James were in the savior category. They didn't need the money. But maybe she was wrong about them. Then again, maybe she wasn't. How much could you really piece together from glistening eyes, food faces, and takeout?

"Sure," Morgan said. "Let's eat and celebrate whatever mystery occasion we're celebrating."

"We just want it to be a surprise, until it isn't," Katie said.

Morgan looked at Eli with wide eyes as they entered the dining room. She mouthed, "What the heck?"

Eli shrugged. He did a lot of shrugging.

It wasn't your average takeout. That much was clear as soon as Katie and James started to plate the food from the containers. They were using what Morgan figured were the good plates, not the ones they'd eaten off previously.

It looked like the china you'd use for Christmas dinner or Thanksgiving or something—gleaming white and outlined in gold. And it wasn't just the plates. Katie had brought out the good silverware and crystal—old-fashioned glasses with snowflake designs on them. Each of the fancy plates ended up being filled, appropriately, with fancy food. Katie announced what they would be eating like she was a server at a restaurant reciting the specials. Salad with field greens, cucumber, feta, red onion, sunflower seeds, cranberries, wild rice. Bison chili with seasonal beans, veggies, sweet corn, and shredded cheese. And, last but not least, traditional bannock.

It was most certainly nothing like McDonald's. If Katie hadn't told her it was takeout, Morgan would have believed the meal to be homemade. It looked, she had to admit, amazing. The first thing she did was pull off a piece of bannock, slather it with butter, and pop it into her mouth. Now, she was by no means a bannock aficionado—she had eaten it only rarely, as a matter of fact—but this tasted good. The last time she'd had some was in September, during the school's Orange Shirt Day, when the student body honored the First Nations children who had attended residential schools. Over lunch, everybody had been given bannock. It seemed to Morgan on both occasions that butter was key.

Once Morgan took a bite, it was like everybody else was okay to start eating. For several minutes, they all dug in to their dinner and didn't talk. The only sounds were knives and forks scraping against plates, and chewing. The chewing reminded Morgan of the crunching sound she'd heard that morning, which reminded her of walking through snow, which reminded her of cold wind, which reminded her of the little gusts of air that had mysteriously brushed her face in the attic.

"Is the food okay?" Katie asked hopefully.

Morgan nodded while she finished a mouthful of chili. "Yeah."

"You don't have to like it, really," Katie said. "I want us to be honest with each other."

"I do." Morgan stopped herself from adding that it wasn't like Katie had cooked it, and why did dinner have to be about trust anyway?

"It's good," Eli said, backing Morgan up.

From the look on her foster parents' faces, Eli's approval meant more to them. For that, she couldn't blame them. She'd heard them talking in their bedroom at night—James didn't know how to whisper—about how to connect with him, how to make him feel at home. Why did they always seem to want her and Eli to feel at home? This wasn't their home. They were just staying here.

One day, they wouldn't be.

"I got it from this Indigenous-owned restaurant downtown," Katie said. "I wanted . . ."

Please don't say anything about feeling at home, Morgan thought. She felt a spark of flame in her chest. It was about to get warm, then hot. She closed her eyes tight, bracing herself.

But Katie must've picked up on the signal. It wasn't subtle. "Well anyway."

"We're glad you like it," James said.

The table remained silent for the duration of the meal, as though, more than savoring the food, Katie and James were savoring the small victories of having Eli speak and both kids liking the meal.

Once they'd all finished, Katie and James cleared all the dishes from the table. Morgan even offered to help, but James quickly told her it wasn't necessary, which made her suspicious. They disappeared into the kitchen for a long time without reemerging.

Even more suspicious.

Morgan waited with nervous anticipation. She and Eli glanced at each other intermittently. He looked nervous. He was probably waiting to see if she could hold it together. She wondered what could be next, after an "Indigenous meal." A gift? What kind of gift? A braid of sweetgrass? A dream catcher? One of those tobacco ties she'd seen on Orange Shirt Day? But she was pretty sure only Elders got tobacco offerings.

Eli would know.

"Hey," she whispered, as if talking about anything Indigenous was a secret.

"Yeah?" he whispered back.

"Tobacco," she stated, as though the word was an entire question.

"Yeah?"

"Is that just for Elders? Like, you give it to them when you want to ask them questions, right?" she asked.

"It's like"—he sat forward in his chair—"when you're asking somebody to share knowledge, you offer them tobacco. It doesn't have to be an Elder."

"But *they*, like, Katie and James, wouldn't give me tobacco or anything, right?" she asked.

"Not unless they want you to share knowledge," he said.

"Well"—Morgan crossed her arms and leaned back in her chair—"I don't know anything about stuff like that, so they're in for a surprise."

"You don't even know they're going to do that!" Eli shout-whispered. He looked even more worried now. "Are you going to freak if they bring out something Native?" he asked, making air quotes while saying *Native*.

"I didn't freak about the bannock, did I?" Morgan said. "I just shut up and ate it."

"Yeah, but—"

Katie and James entered the dining room, and James was carrying a cake that looked like a birthday cake. He placed it in front of Morgan, and she avoided reading what was written on the top, mostly so that she wouldn't get annoyed.

But there was more.

"Before we have dessert," Katie announced, "we have a little gift for you."

They actually did *get me tobacco or something*, Morgan thought. She saw Katie's hands shaking and prepared herself to make it through the tobacco offering without *looking* like she had any negative emotions about it.

"Wait!" Morgan decided to save them from her getting food face–level mad. "Please tell me what this is all about. Like, why doesn't Eli get something? You don't want him to be sad but you're totally leaving him out."

"I'm okay," Eli said, sounding like he wanted no part of any of this.

"Well . . ." Katie exchanged a look with James, who nodded at her. "We wanted to do something because you've been here for two months now."

"Two months today," James added, as though Morgan needed the math explained.

But maybe she did. She hadn't kept track of when she'd arrived and certainly would never have kept track to celebrate the date. "So we're celebrating." Morgan tried to swallow the burning in her chest. "Our anniversary." *Like we're dating*, Morgan continued in her head.

"That's right," Katie said.

"Not in a weird way," James said.

Oh, it was weird, but Morgan also kept this to herself. "Why two months? Why not one month?"

"It just felt like maybe you needed something nice done for you today," Katie said.

"So this *is* because of the food face," Morgan said. "You know, I would've been, like, fine if you didn't make my food into a happy face, right?"

"That was just a coincidence," James said, obviously trying to avoid another blowup.

"*Are* you fine, though?" Katie asked.

This question hung in the air until Katie placed a box on the table beside the cake. It had black wrapping paper with two ribbons, one red and one yellow, which met at the top of the package under a pretty white bow. They were the same colors as the medicine wheel Morgan had seen at school.

Morgan took a deep breath. *Remain calm. So what, they're celebrating your two-month anniversary with them. It's cringe-worthy, but there are worse things in the world. Climate change, for example. That's worse.*

Katie and James looked hopeful.

Eli looked scared.

Katie slid the gift closer towards Morgan. "Open it."

"Okay," Morgan said. "Sure."

Morgan pulled off the bow, slid off the ribbons, and ripped open the wrapping paper to reveal a shoebox. The box read "Manitobah Mukluks." She lifted the lid and saw a brand-new pair of moccasins. They were mostly black, with black leather and black fur around the opening and a dark shade of gray over the top with some intricate white beadwork.

Morgan closed her eyes and focused on her breathing.

"Do you like them?" Katie asked.

Morgan kept her eyes closed as long as she could.

"Morgan?" James said.

Morgan shook her head quickly. She needed a minute. *Just accept them and put them on your stupid feet. Let it go.*

Katie said, "We thought you could just wear them around the house. I know the hardwood down here gets cold in the morning, so it would be comfortable. And in the winter—"

"You can actually wear them outside, instead of boots," James said. "They're called Wool Tipi."

"Wool Tipi," Morgan repeated. Still breathing.

"We wanted to make you feel more at home," Katie said.

Morgan slammed a flat palm against the table. "Okay!" She opened her eyes. Katie and James looked stunned. Frozen. Eyes wide. Eli looked like a balloon that had air seeping out of it. "Let me get this straight," she said, trying to lower her voice. "You thought that giving me something *cultural* as a totally lame two-month anniversary celebration, from a place I was taken from, would make me feel more at home *here*?"

"We don't want you to feel *disconnected* from your culture, that's all," James said.

"I don't even *know* my culture." Morgan put both hands against her chest, and she could feel her heart pounding. "I've literally been away from my home since I was a toddler. Being a kid with no real home? With no real parents? Accepting the fact that there probably won't be a three- or four-month anniversary with a cake and moccasins? *That's* my culture."

"No, it's not," Eli said. "Who you are is still inside you."

"*Shut up*, Eli, you're not helping," Morgan said.

"He's right, though," James said. "We thought some of this might help you reconnect with—"

"We've read that, as foster parents, we should try to expose you to your culture." Katie looked about ready to burst into tears. "We don't want to make the same mistakes that have been made in the past."

"Well, unless you can, like, go into the quantum realm, go back in time, and stop my mom from getting *rid* of me, I . . ." Morgan stopped. She placed both palms flat on the table to keep herself steady. "*Everything*'s a mistake."

"Your mom didn't get rid of you," Katie said.

"Did she tell you that?" Morgan asked through clenched teeth. "What are you guys, Facebook friends?"

"No, just no mother would—"

"You're not a mother so how would you know?!" Morgan

stood up. She glanced from Katie to James to Eli. "Maybe you should read one of *my* books instead of whatever you've been reading, because trying to fix things, trying to fix *me*, really is a fantasy!"

She turned away from the table, from the people and the cake and the moccasins, and started towards the stairs.

"Morgan, come back here and sit down, please." James said.

"No," Katie said to him. "Just let her go. Give her space."

Let her go. Those three words echoed in her mind. *Let her go.* Morgan was sure that's exactly what they'd do, especially after a day like today.

SEVEN

Morgan sprinted up two flights of stairs to the second floor, slammed the door behind her, and stopped in the middle of the hallway. She was out of breath, but not from the stairs. Her chest was heaving and she couldn't catch her breath because she was crying so hard. Each time she wiped her cheeks, they were soaked again, instantly. If her head were against her pillow right now, and the scene of the blizzard had burst back into her mind, she wouldn't be trudging through the snow, she'd be running through it. Her heart was racing.

She'd run up the stairs with the intention of going to her bedroom, packing her clothes, and leaving. They were just going to kick her out now anyway. She knew it. She'd been removed from houses before. She'd run away from houses before. One way or another, with every house, eventually she would be gone. And it would be the same here.

She bent over, put her hands on her knees, and stared at the carpet.

"You jerk," she forced out between sobs. "You stupid jerk. Those stupid jerks."

She looked up. She could hardly see her room through the tears. The open door, and what lay inside, was just a blurry, dark vortex. Like, if she went in, she'd be swallowed whole and never come out again. She shook her head at the thought, looked down again, and the tears she'd shaken loose fell to the carpet, making tiny, dark blotches in the fabric. She felt like they might swallow her whole too. She felt like everything might, that everything was darkness, and maybe it was better that way, to just get sucked up into it and vanish.

"No," she said, panting.

She didn't want that. She didn't want to leave somewhere else. She'd left too many places. She was tired. She couldn't catch her breath from crying; she couldn't ever catch her breath, just from life in the foster care system. And Katie and James, they were alright. They were good. She'd not had foster parents like them before. Yes, they'd fed her bannock. And yes, they'd given her moccasins. But Katie had said they were trying, and weren't they? Was it so bad? Who'd tried to connect with her like that before? Even if she didn't want the moccasins, was that their fault? Maybe. Maybe not.

She wanted to pull her head off, it was spinning so hard from the confusion.

"What just happened?" she whispered to herself.

Then, out of nowhere, Eli's face was in her mind. How he was yesterday, how he was today. He'd changed so much, just in that time. He was talking. She was talking.

He'd asked why she was so angry, and she knew that she was. It was like he knew her as well as she thought she knew him. Was she just going to leave him now? What would happen to him? What would happen to her?

She tried to even out her breathing. Tears kept dripping onto the carpet. On the first floor, dead silence. She pictured them all, sitting there in stunned silence. She replayed what had just happened. Slamming the table. Shouting. Telling Katie that she wasn't a mother. Morgan buried her fingers in her hair and pulled. She wanted to scream, but didn't. Instead, she turned away from the carpet, turned away from her room, and started running.

She kept running as far as she could run without running away.

Another two flights of stairs, and she was in the attic. She looked frantically around the large room with its broken walls and piles of debris. There had to be somewhere to go, somewhere to hide, just for a little while. So that she could gather herself. So that when they came to get her, to give her away, they couldn't find her.

She scanned the room, from left to right, from the place where she read most nights when Katie and James were asleep, all the way across, to the painted-over door.

That was it.

Nobody had been in there for . . . ever. Forever was probable. And because of that, if she was able to open it, get to the other side, it would be her *real* secret place. And Eli could come in. Of course he could come in.

But she had to open the door first.

Morgan gripped the doorknob, turned it, and pulled.

The door refused to budge. She put both hands on the knob, braced her feet against the baseboard, and tried again. There might have been some give, she might have imagined it, but either way, the door looked just the way it had before. The paint, layered over the door and the frame, remained intact. In an effort that she knew would be fruitless, born of frustration, she lunged into the door with her shoulder, twice, but she only hurt herself.

"Come on!"

She stared at the door from top to bottom, waiting for a thought to come to her. Then her eyes drifted to some screws and nails and shards of wood littered over the plywood floor, remnants of the ongoing, endless renovation.

Tools!

She ran to the other side of the room, found the tool bag, and fished through it until she found what she was looking for: a box cutter. All she needed to do was cut around the door and break the paint seal. Once that was done, she'd be able to open it, no problem. If she was able to do it so it wasn't noticeable, great. But James never came up here anyway, so it might not matter.

Morgan started at the bottom left corner and worked her way up. The paint was hard and thick, and it felt like she was sawing through wood. Still, as the minutes passed, she made progress. Up the side, across the top, and down the opposite side. In less than ten minutes, she'd pushed the blade through the last bit of paint, and she stood up to regard her work triumphantly. Semi-triumphantly. Anybody would totally see that the paint had been cut away.

She'd worry about that later.

Morgan put her hand on the doorknob again, twisted, and pulled. The door jolted like it was gasping to life as the latch bolt released. She pulled the door open and was greeted by a waft of stale air.

She couldn't see anything inside the room. It was pitch-black. She stood a few feet from the dark space and stared into it. She waited for her eyes to adjust, but the room stubbornly remained a mystery until she turned her phone's flashlight on. Inch by inch, left to right, the room revealed itself.

Some mystery.

It was just more unfinished attic space, about the size of her bedroom. The wall to her left followed the slope of the roof, while the one on the right was just beams and ply-wood (the other side of it being the stairwell). The wall facing Morgan showed the brick outline of the house chimney. Courageous with the flashlight, Morgan entered the room, sat down facing the sloped wall, and propped up her phone against the wall at her side.

And that was that. She would stay here until the phone died.

Morgan hugged her knees to her chest and buried her face between them. Acting like an ostrich again. She tried not to think about anything, but it didn't work. The entire day kept forcing itself into her head. Mostly breakfast and dinner.

"I should just not eat again, problem solved," she grumbled.

And the tears came back. The only difference now was that she wasn't sobbing. She was too tired to sob. The tears just kind of fell, and Morgan didn't much care for them to stop. She was also too tired for that.

After a while, she heard the door open to the second floor, and footsteps leading to one of the bedrooms. Katie's, she guessed. The same footsteps started up the stairs on their way to the attic.

"Great," she whispered, without lifting her head.

She knew she'd left the door open, which defeated the whole purpose of having a secret room. What kind of secret room was it if you forgot to shut the secret door?

When the footsteps reached the top of the last flight, she busily wiped her eyes and cheeks against her knees, removing the evidence of her tears. The footsteps stopped at the attic door and she looked up to find Eli standing there, looking at her, carrying his drawing pad.

"Hey," he said.

"Hey," she said, giving her eyes one last wipe, this time with her sleeve. She sniffled, just in case there was any snot coming out of her nose. "How'd you know I was up here?"

"Everybody knows you're up here," he said. "You were loud."

"Oh." Morgan buried her face again. "Are they mad?"

"I think you're getting a pass," he said.

"I don't deserve a pass," she said. "I'm a jerk."

"Sometimes maybe."

She heard him enter the room and walk towards her, and she felt the floor compress with each footstep. She felt his shoulder brush against hers as he sat beside her. She kept her head down. She didn't want him to leave, but she didn't want to say anything. He must have known that, because he didn't say anything either. They just sat there on the floor, in the secret room, as the battery life of her cell dwindled.

Sometime later, Morgan sighed.

"The last place I was at," she said, "they used to tell me I was part of their family. I was there for almost two years, I think. They had two kids, a girl and a boy, and a dog too. Juby. That was the dog's name. Did you ever have a dog, Eli?"

He nodded.

"What was its name?" she asked.

"Red," he whispered.

"Their family, my foster mom's parents, lived in another town. It was, like, three hours away. They'd go visit every other weekend. My foster parents, the kids, Juby. But I never got to go. They'd put me in respite care, get another family to look after me while they were gone." Morgan wiped a tear away from her cheek with her knee. "They took the dog but not me." Finally, she looked at Eli. "The last time they went away, I took off. Nobody found me for a few days. I don't know when they even started looking." She chuckled. "I wasn't hiding; I was just running, you know?"

"Yeah," he said.

She ran her hands through her hair. Pushed loose strands behind her ear. She smiled at Eli, because he looked like he wanted to cry too. "I think I wanted them to want me. Funny, right? I wanted them to want me, so I ran away." She shook her head. "Stupid. Anyway"—she clapped her hands to snap them both out of it—"they didn't, and here I am."

"You're not going to run away from here, are you?" Eli asked.

"No," she assured him, "I'm not going to run away."

"Good."

"I'm just going to move up here for, like, ever."

60

"They're not going to get rid of you."

"Maybe."

"But if you're going to stay up here, I made you a house-warming gift." Eli picked up his drawing pad from the floor. He opened it to the first page. He was being dramatic about it. The big paper was facing him, and Morgan couldn't see what he'd drawn. She tried to snatch it from him, but he pulled it away.

"You don't tease a girl who's just had a meltdown, you know," she said.

"Okay, fine." He turned the paper around to reveal his work.

Morgan gasped when she saw it. Not that it was scary or shocking. But it was such a wonderful picture. "When did you even draw this?"

"Katie and James went into the kitchen and were whispering to each other for a long time," he said. "I got bored."

"Can I?" Morgan reached with both hands for the drawing pad.

Eli let her take it.

She placed the pad on her lap, picked up her cellphone, and shone the light on the drawing so she could see every detail. An animal being—Morgan wasn't sure what kind of animal—was walking through a field, its arm raised to shield its face from the wind and whipping snow. Funny Its tracks were coming from a village in the distance. It wasn't going towards it. The village, all the way across the field, was nestled against a forest that stretched from one end of the drawing to the other. There were lights in the houses. As she looked intently at the illustration, she started to hear the same beats from that morning, as if it wasn't a drawing at all, as if the beast was walking right towards her. Then she realized that she wasn't hearing the animal walking. Again, the sound was just her heart pounding.

"There was no wind," Eli said.

"Huh?" Morgan tore her eyes away from the picture, but kept the pad open and on her lap.

"When I was drawing it," he said, "there was no wind. Maybe . . ."

"Maybe what?" she asked.

"Maybe it wasn't coming from the paper," he admitted.

"And you're sad about that?" she asked, because he did look sad. "You wanted your paper to be haunted?"

He shook his head. "I guess not."

"Exactly," she said. "Magic is best kept to books. Plus, magic drawing pads that shoot cold air? That's lame."

She held the pad up, inspected the drawing again, and this time heard no heartbeat, no footsteps through snow. And there was no cold air coming into the real world. Everything that it was was right there in front of her. The only mystery was the animal, but that was just because she didn't know it. She asked Eli.

"That's a fisher," he said.

"You saw them where you live"—she corrected herself—"lived?"

Maybe she shouldn't have. He slumped.

"Yeah, I saw them out in the bush, when I was hunting with . . ."

"With?"

"Never mind. I saw them."

"Did this come from a story you know?"

"No," he said, "I just kept drawing it. I didn't know what I was drawing. I had this picture in my head all day."

Morgan held the drawing closer to her face. "I think I did too," she said absently, not really to Eli.

"You did?" he asked.

"Well, *I* was walking instead of the fisher, but *still*," she said. "Weird."

The creature's black eyes were watching her, and it was creepy. It was like when you know somebody is staring at you. Goose pimples rose on her arms. She moved the drawing pad from side to side, up and down, but the fisher wouldn't take its eyes off her. She remembered how Mrs. Bignell had shown them that the Mona Lisa doesn't stop looking at you, no matter where you are in the room. She'd taped up a poster of the painting and had the kids move from corner to corner, and all around the room. She was right. This fisher was the animal version of the Mona Lisa.

The odd thing about it was that she didn't quite want it to look away.

"We should put it up on the wall," she said.

"I didn't literally mean that it was for this room." Eli looked around at the place Morgan had discovered, unimpressed.

Morgan stood up and started pacing around the small room. "If Katie and James know that I'm up here, even if they're not going to kick us out, we need a new, even more secret place . . . and this is it!"

"*This* is our new secret place?" he repeated.

"Imagine the possibilities!" For the first time all day she felt excited. "We'll bring some comforters up here, pillows.

I'll bring some books, you bring . . . pencils and stuff, I guess. Oh! We could even get those lights that strap to our heads!"

While Morgan paced around the room, she saw Eli watching her, and it looked to her as though he was, as instructed, trying to imagine the possibilities. Really, she wasn't asking much. Blankets and pillows. Imagining that couldn't have been difficult.

"Okay," he said. "Sure."

"Yes!" Morgan jumped and clapped her hands. "Now, first things first. Can I take this drawing out of the pad?"

Eli nodded.

"Thanks." Morgan pulled the drawing out carefully, then looked around for the perfect place. She pressed it against each of the walls, sliding it around on every imaginable spot, but settled on the slanting wall, the roof of the house. She positioned it so that it was centered exactly between the roof and the floor, wall to wall. "Can you hold it just like this?"

Eli stood up and held the drawing in place.

"Good. *Great.*" Morgan placed her phone back against the opposite wall, slanting it upward so light showered over the illustration. "Hold it there."

She ran across the attic, dug into the tool bag again, and found a staple gun she'd seen earlier when retrieving the box cutter. Moments later, she was back in their secret place. She positioned the staple gun over the top right corner of the paper, squeezed it, and *thwack.* A staple shot into the wood, affixing the paper to the wall.

A gust of air blew out of the paper, much stronger than before. Morgan's entire head of hair blew backward as if a hair dryer had been turned on to maximum power.

But as quickly as the gust came, it was gone.

"Whoa," Morgan said.

"That came from the paper," Eli stated.

"It totally did."

They stared at the picture, then at each other. Eli nodded at Morgan, giving her permission to add another staple. Another gust of wind, this one stronger still. And it was cold wind. It stung Morgan's cheeks, already raw from crying.

"This can't be happening," she said.

"And why now? Why not when I was drawing downstairs?" he asked.

"Good question. Maybe, okay, don't think this is cheesy, but maybe we have to be together?"

"But why?"

"I don't know!" Morgan threw her hand in the air. "I'm trying to think like this is a fantasy book."

"Maybe we have to be in the attic?"

"It's kind of sweeter if it's us, not a room. Just saying."

"Sorry?"

"Just kidding. I'm trying not to freak out—these things don't happen in real life!"

"Oh."

Morgan pressed the staple gun against another corner of the drawing. "Should I?"

"Yeah."

Thwack.

An avalanche of freezing air burst through the paper and pushed both of them back, almost to the opposite wall. And then it was gone. Morgan's hair was crazy, like she'd just woken up or stuck a finger in an electrical socket. Even Eli's hair, usually perfectly braided, slick and beautiful, had strands blown out of place.

The attic was cold. The wind had come out like a lightning bolt, abruptly stopping each time, and it left behind a lingering chill. There was one corner left to staple.

Morgan placed the staple gun against the last corner.

"Ready?" she asked.

"Ready," he said.

Thwack.

The blizzard in the drawing, once just pencil lines, stormed into the attic room. The kids stumbled backwards against the wall. Morgan tried to move to the side, out of the way of the wind, but there was no escaping it, and this time it was unrelenting. It wasn't just wind either. Snow was pouring into the room, so fast and hard that it stung against Morgan's skin. She raised her arm in front of her face to shield it from the onslaught. Eli did the same. Within seconds, the floor was covered in white flakes.

Morgan peeked over her arm to look at the paper fastened to the wall. It had been a drawing, but not anymore. Now it was a window. But the window didn't open to the world outside the house; it opened to the world that Eli had created, the world that Morgan had pictured that morning.

She could see the blizzard, both in the attic and in the picture. She could see the near-endless field of snow. She could see, just barely, the tree line far in the distance. She could see shimmering lights, like tiny stars, from the village.

She could see the fisher.

The animal being was walking towards them. At first slowly, then it broke into a run. Snow kicked up behind it. Morgan screamed. Eli rushed forward, ripped the paper away from the wood, and the other world was gone.

"It's ice-cold!" Eli said, dropping it.

It floated to the ground like a snowflake.

Morgan and Eli stood there, staring at each other for a long while, until Morgan whispered, "Pick up the drawing."

It was on the floor, and the melting snow was beginning to dampen the paper.

"I just let it go; why do I have to do it?" he asked.

"It's *your* drawing," she said. "Plus, I'm older."

Eli kicked at the drawing first. A few snowflakes coughed out of it, but nothing more. He bent over, tapped at it a few times, then picked it up. He turned it over slowly to reveal that the picture was exactly as he'd drawn it. The snow. The trees. The village. Only now the fisher seemed closer than he had before, and stuck in mid-run.

Coming right at them.

EIGHT

"Did he see us?" Morgan took the drawing from Eli and inspected it. The fisher was definitely closer. And more than that, one arm was extended out, reaching for them. "Oh my god, he *did* see us!" She kept expecting snow and wind to erupt from the page at any moment. Her hands were shaking. From the cold, from the shock of it all, from the thought of some animal being sprinting at them.

She handed the drawing back to Eli, too freaked out to hold it any longer. It was like a scene from a horror movie.

Eli's hands were not shaking at all.

"Aren't you scared?" she asked.

He was looking at the drawing, and not at Morgan. He ran his fingers across the surface of it. "It's still cold."

"Eli." Morgan snapped her fingers to get his attention.

"Huh?"

"I asked if you were scared," she said. "Why aren't you scared? This is a little crazy, no?"

"It reminds me of home," he said.

"Your home is like Hoth?"

"Hoth?"

"Are you serious?" she said. "The Rebel Alliance's secret base? *Star Wars?* Ring a bell?"

Eli shook his head.

"Well, if that"—she pointed at the drawing from a safe distance—"reminds you of home, trust me: your home is like Hoth." She picked up her phone and used it to guide them out of the secret room. "And that *thing* is the abominable snowman creature that captured Luke."

"That's not a thing," Eli said. "It's a fisher. In Cree, the word for fisher is *ochek*."

Morgan turned on her heels so fast that her hair whipped her cheeks. "Yeah? What's the word for *did you not just see a portal open to another world and that* ochek *running at us like it wanted to kill us?*"

Her feet were wet from the floor. She took off her socks and wrung them out.

"There's no word for that in Cree," Eli said.

"Duh," Morgan said. "It's called sarcasm."

She took one step down the first flight of stairs, but he put a hand on her shoulder. She stopped.

"What?" she said.

"Aren't you curious?"

"I'm a little too freaked out to be curious, Eli," she said. "We just saw a picture come to life. And it's freaking me out that you're not freaked out."

She kept walking down the stairs.

"But wouldn't you want to go through the picture? If you could?" he asked.

This time, she stopped on her own. "You mean, if there wasn't a humanoid animal running at us? Would I want to go through a picture into another world?"

"Doesn't that happen in your books?" he asked.

"Yes," she stated plainly. "That happens in my *fiction* books." She leaned in close to him to drive home her point. "Did you consider that he might have been mad? I mean, we were, like, humans trying to come onto his land."

"Kind of like in real life too," he said.

"Whatever." Morgan ran up the stairs and snatched the picture from his hands. "We should burn it. Make sure that thing doesn't, I don't know, crawl out and kill us in our sleep."

Eli, in turn, grabbed it from her. "We aren't burning it!"

He gripped the picture with both hands, in case she tried to take it again. He wouldn't look away from it, and when she shone her flashlight on him, she could see that he didn't look curious anymore, but sad. It reminded him of home, and he wasn't anywhere near home. He was here, in this attic, in this house, in the middle of some upper-middle-class neighborhood, in this city. It wasn't long ago that he'd been in his own community.

She sat down on the top step.

"I don't remember my home," she said. "I wouldn't even call it home."

She wrapped her arms around her body. Now that the shock of what they'd seen, and heard, had begun to wear off, she noticed that her shirt was wet, and she felt cold.

"It's not the blizzard that's like home," Eli said, "or the *ochek.*" He sat down beside her. She looked at him. He smiled. She smiled back. "It's the open space. All the room. There

70

was this field behind my house that was, like, forever long, and I could just play in it all day. Even when I was lost, I wasn't lost."

Morgan put her arm around Eli. She didn't try to take the picture again. She even looked at it. Tried to see what he saw, remember what he remembered.

"Okay, we won't burn it," she said. "But can we leave it up here, in the room? Nothing will happen to it."

"Promise?" he asked. "You won't come back up here and throw it out later?"

"Promise," she assured him. "And if the fisher tries to crawl out of the picture—can I remind you how crazy this all sounds?—we'll cross that bridge when we come to it."

"It won't," he said.

"How do you know?"

"Because we did something. I don't think the portal will . . . open . . . unless we do the same things again."

"Staple-gun it to the wall?"

"Maybe."

Morgan put her hand on her face and shook her head. "We must be sleeping." She pinched her thigh, then her arm, several times. Her skin was as numb as it was cold, but she could still feel the pinches. She didn't wake up in bed, her ear pressed against the pillow so she could hear her heartbeat. She remained on the steps, sitting beside Eli, both of them staring at a picture that had just come alive.

"We just opened a portal to another world," she said.

"We should go there."

"We should go . . . what? No! Are you crazy?" Morgan did snatch away the drawing this time, but not to burn it.

She walked back into the attic, tossed the picture into the secret room, then slammed the door.

"Maybe the *ochek* needed us!" Eli pleaded. "Maybe it wasn't running after us to kill us! It was stuck in that blizzard, right?"

"It wasn't stuck in the blizzard. There was a village behind it, remember? You drew the picture!"

"What if we're supposed to go to the other side?" he asked. "You said it yourself: it's a portal to another world. Why would it open *now*? With us right *here*? We can't just ignore that."

"Oh yes, we can," she said. "We'll seal this place back up and pretend like we never found it. I like my fantasy worlds in books."

"I don't want to pretend that we never found it!"

"You just want to pretend it's your home because you don't have one anymore!"

The attic fell deathly silent. Through the door to their secret room Morgan could hear drops of water land on the plywood from the sloped ceiling. Snow, left over from the blizzard, melting.

"Eli," she whispered. "I'm *so* sorry." Of all the things she'd done today, this was by far the worst. "I . . . I was just scared."

Instead of answering, instead of looking up at Morgan, Eli just got up and left, with his head down. She heard his steps on the stairs to the second floor. Morgan waited a moment longer, then followed behind him. By the time she walked into the hallway, he'd already shut the door to his bedroom.

Morgan went to her room. She shut the door, took off her damp clothing, put on a pair of sweats and a ratty old T-shirt, and collapsed onto her bed. She lay on her stomach with her face pushed hard into the pillow, crying, until it was as damp as the clothing she'd taken off.

"Morgan?"

It was Katie. How much time had passed? Minutes? An hour?

Morgan hadn't been thinking about the portal, or about the fisher, just about Eli and what she'd said to him. How could she have said that, like she'd never gone through what he was going through right now? She was scared, like she'd told him. Scared, and the more she thought of it, jealous. That he remembered his home, and she didn't. She'd never thought she wanted to.

Morgan didn't say anything, but she felt Katie sit down at the foot of her bed. She looked up to see that Katie was holding the shoebox, and the first thing Katie did was put it on the ground and slide it across the carpet until it was flush against the wall.

"Have the moccasins been repurposed as a peace offering?" Morgan asked, staring out the window at a streetlight. "Because if we're being all 'Indigenous,' I think I've learned something about smoking a pipe for that."

It got quiet. So quiet Morgan thought she could hear Eli's pencil scraping against paper.

"I don't know why I say things like that," Morgan whispered.

"I, uhhh . . ." Katie shifted her body to face Morgan. Morgan could see the movement out of the corner of her eye. "I googled Manitobah Mukluks. There are people who try to profit from Indigenous culture. You know, like gift shops in small towns that sell dream catchers or something? You hang them on your rearview mirror . . . stuff like that. Those people have bad intentions."

Morgan turned towards Katie slightly.

Katie went on. "But Manitobah Mukluks, that's a company owned and operated by Indigenous people. That doesn't mean you have to wear them, Morgan." Katie learned forward and rubbed her palms against her knees. Were her palms sweating? "I don't think I'm saving you by fostering you. You're a strong young woman. You don't need saving. I'm just . . . James and I . . . we want to make sure you're not . . ." She rubbed her face. "Well, I'm just one of those good-intentioned settlers, okay?"

Morgan turned onto her back and propped herself up on a pillow.

"At the school where I teach, there isn't a lot of diversity. The neighborhood's a lot like this one, so . . . you get what I'm saying. Anyway, in my grade five class, there was this one girl. A beautiful girl. She's Indigenous. She looked sad all the time, and scared. One day, halfway through the year, I guess after she started to trust me, she told me what she'd gone through. She was in care." Katie shook her head, wiped at her cheek, at a tear that had fallen. "*Care.*"

"What'd she say?" Morgan asked.

Katie shook her head again, like Morgan shouldn't know, or Katie couldn't say. "I thought, if I could just show a kid love, you know? If I could give a kid a good home . . ."

"Then you'd somehow be helping that girl?"

"Maybe." She nodded. "Or I could just be helping you."

Morgan looked Katie over in the quiet that followed. She couldn't have been older than thirty. Her light-brown hair was tied back into a loose ponytail that had been tighter at dinner. She was wearing gray yoga pants and a thin, black cardigan that she was hugging around her body. Her glasses were sliding towards the tip of her nose.

"Those moccasins," Katie said, "the bannock . . ." She chuckled softly, a gentle self-admonishment, Morgan imagined. "I thought I should try to connect you with your culture, that maybe it would make things better. For you."

Morgan sat up, leaned forward on her elbows. "Those moccasins would've been perfect for Eli, you know. He's got himself figured out. He's Indigenous. Probably goes to ceremonies and all that. I don't think I even want to be Indigenous. I grew up white, in all these white homes. I'm *not* Indigenous anymore."

Katie spoke carefully and quietly. "Does doing all that make him more Indigenous than you?"

Morgan shrugged. She didn't know. She didn't know what to say.

"Tell me what I can do," Katie said. "That's part of how I can learn, if you could just—"

"Just treat me like I'm any other human girl, that's it. I don't need, you know, to wear those"—she pointed at the gift Katie and James had got her—"or hang dream catchers from my window, or smudge every morning, or whatever else. Just treat me like a girl."

Katie shuffled up the bed, closer to Morgan. Closer, but not too close. She put her hand on Morgan's foot. "I like you, Morgan. James and I both do. We don't want to lose you."

"Even if I act crazy?" Morgan asked, trying to keep the tears deep down in her stomach. She'd cried enough today.

Katie smiled reassuringly. "Nothing you can do can make us want you gone, Morgan. And speaking of humans, of being a girl, girls . . . teens . . . can do that sometimes. I was a girl once, you know, believe it or not. I did way worse than slam my palm on a table or make an adult's breakfast into a mad face."

"It was just the whole day." Morgan thought of every little thing she'd done, that she wished she hadn't.

Katie didn't say anything. She sat there for a moment, tapped Morgan on the foot a couple of times, then got up from the bed.

"I won't run away," Morgan blurted out before Katie had left the bedroom and closed the door.

"Then I'll see you in the morning." Katie turned back one last time. "And no faces on your breakfast plate, moccasins, bannock . . ."

"Actually, I kind of like bannock," Morgan said. "With lots of butter. And jam sometimes."

Katie chuckled and shut the door.

Morgan turned onto her side, stared out the window, and stayed like that until the house was dark and quiet. No movement. No snoring. She wanted to go see Eli and apologize to him. Tell him: okay, if the portal works again, if it wasn't some crazy mind-meld hallucination they had simultaneously, they could check it out. Go through it. Just a few steps. And only if the fisher wasn't there. If it was running at them again, no deal.

But it had been a long day, and in thinking about all this, she fell asleep.

NINE

Morgan was having something between a dream and a nightmare. She was standing outside a window to a small room. Not any room in Katie and James's house, but still familiar. A place she'd not been in for a long time. Somehow, she knew that. A winter storm was blowing around her. She put a hand on the cold glass, and as soon as she did, she heard footsteps in the snow behind her. She turned around to see the fisher appear out of the blizzard.

When their eyes met, he charged towards her.

"No!"

Morgan jolted awake, but the cold followed her. She curled the sheets around her body and tried to gather in as much heat as she could. Soon, the remnants of the dream would pass and she would feel warm again. It had felt so real, and when that happened, she knew she'd feel stuck in the dream for a while before coming to her senses.

But as seconds turned to minutes and Morgan felt more and more awake, she didn't feel any less cold. *I've got the flu,* she thought, and decided that she would get up and make herself tea. She checked the time on her cellphone: just before three in the morning. She'd been asleep for only, like, two hours. The night light behind her headboard threw a white halo across the floor and walls.

Morgan left her phone on the floor and sat up.

The hairs on her arms were standing up. She rubbed them vigorously. The only solution, before making a nice cup of hot tea, was to bundle up. She grabbed a thick hoodie from her closet, slipped on a pair of socks, and even, albeit reluctantly, put on the moccasins. It turned out to be a good choice. When Morgan opened the door and stepped into the hallway, she felt even colder.

"What the . . . ?" she whispered.

The first thing Morgan noticed was that the door to the attic was open, and all the cold air was coming from up there. Her heart started pounding.

"Oh no," she whispered.

She rushed over to Katie and James's bedroom and opened the door. They were huddled together under their duvet, sound asleep. Good. Morgan shut their door quietly, then ran into Eli's room, right up to his bed. She threw the comforter off to find that he wasn't there. She checked the rest of his room, refusing to believe that he'd done what she knew by now he must have done. He wasn't anywhere. Not under the bed, not in the closet.

There was only one place left to look.

Morgan ran up the stairs, taking them two at a time, to the attic. The door to their secret room was wide open. It had probably been left ajar, and the wind from the storm had pushed it all the way open. The cold had flooded into the attic, down the stairs, and filled the second floor.

It didn't look like their room anymore. It was more like an extension of what they'd seen inside the drawing. Blowing snow had caked against the walls and built up from the floor to above her ankles. She peered through the swirling flakes to see the drawing, stapled back against the sloped wall, which was clearly now a portal to the snow-filled world. She pulled her hood up over her head, stuck her hands into the hoodie's kangaroo pocket, and forged a path through the snow to the opening in the wall. To her relief, the fisher was not there, running at her. But Eli wasn't there either. All she could see through the swirling winds and whipping snow was the field of white. Not even the forest on the horizon or the village.

The storm had gotten worse, if that was even possible.

Morgan stuck her head through the portal and scanned the entire field, but there was nothing to see. An endlessly barren landscape. The wind was severe, kicking up snow and spinning it around in countless miniature tornados. She stared across the field, into the storm, for as long as she could stand, until her skin grew numb. During the briefest of moments, when the wind let up for a second, she did catch a glimpse of the village's lights.

"Eli!" Morgan shouted into the world of white.

She looked at the ground. There were no footprints. Already snowed over.

"Come back!" Morgan screamed, but even as she did, she knew that he'd never be able to hear her. The wind was louder than she could ever hope to be.

Morgan could see only two options: leave him there and wait for him to come back, or go in and get him. The first didn't seem like a choice at all, because what if he never came back? What if he was buried under the snow somewhere? What if he was still walking towards the village? What could he have left with to keep himself warm for the journey? Katie and James had planned to take him out shopping for clothes as winter approached, but they hadn't gone yet.

Then a worse thought came to Morgan: what if Eli hadn't left on his own at all, but the fisher had taken him, just as she'd feared? Either way, this was her fault. She'd said what she'd said, and it had made Eli open the portal and go through it.

"I'm sorry!" she cried out, staring into the blinding white.

There was only one thing Morgan could do: plunge into the void and go after him.

TEN

There was no time to waste. Every second Morgan waited was another moment Eli was in the other world, alone. Maybe dying. And all because she'd said such a horrible thing to him. The only thing she needed to do, before leaving, was think of a way to keep the portal open, so that when she found him, they could come back. At the same time, she needed to stop the cold from coming in. Shutting the door wouldn't help. The blizzard would find a way to keep pushing cold air all through the house. It would have to be done on the other side.

"How would I close the portal on this side if I wasn't just going to tear the paper off?" she asked herself.

She looked away from the secret room and took inventory of the unfinished attic, desperate for an idea. The skeletal walls, the nails and screws and wires all over the floor, the piles of debris with drywall and plywood and . . .

"That's it!"

Morgan gathered up three pieces of plywood that she thought, collectively, would cover the portal, grabbed a handful of nails, and took a hammer from the tool bag. With everything she needed, she stepped inside the secret room and closed the door firmly behind her.

She pocketed the nails, then tossed the hammer and scraps of wood through the opening.

"I guess I'm next," she said.

She would have taken a deep breath, but the air was too cold and the wind too harsh. She could hardly catch her breath, never mind take a nice, long, calming one. She clutched the sides of the portal, braced her feet against the wall, and climbed up, then through, the opening.

Once on the other side, she fell a few feet down, landing in soft, untouched snow. It was like falling into feathers. Morgan stood up and saw that she had come out of a hollow near the base of a massive tree, part of a thickly wooded forest. And while the tree she'd come out of was the thickest and tallest, the others in the forest were no saplings. They looked as old as the earth, and it was incredibly beautiful and familiar. Morgan felt an unmistakable tug in her chest, like *this* was the reason she'd actually come here.

She knew better, though, and shook off whatever pull she felt. She was here for Eli, and by now, he could be lying in the field somewhere, alone and freezing cold. She fished through the deep snow, found the wood and the hammer, and proceeded to nail the flat pieces of wood into the tree and over the portal. This took a long time, long enough that the cold pierced through her hoodie and her hands became frozen stiff. She had to blow on them, or stick them in the kangaroo pocket, between each hammer strike. But eventually the portal was almost fully covered. Now, at least, the attic would be shielded from the blizzard. Katie and James wouldn't notice the cold. But in the morning, if Morgan wasn't back with Eli, they would most certainly notice both their foster kids missing.

Something she'd told Katie echoed in her mind: *"I won't run away."*

She needed to find Eli and figured that she had three hours, at most, until Katie and James woke up. Morgan willed herself to turn away from the forest, the huge tree, and towards the open field. The wind was ferocious, equally cold and strong and loud, and the snow was deep and treacherous. Standing where she was, it already reached her knees. Regardless, she took a step forward, then another. Closer to the village and, hopefully, Eli.

Each step felt harder than the last. The wind was like fire against her exposed face and instantly froze the tears that fell from her eyes. Her muscles and joints ached from the effort of moving through the ever-deepening snow, which crawled inside her moccasins and gnawed at her limbs. Winnipeg, the city she lived in no matter what home she was at, wasn't called "Winterpeg" for nothing. The winters there were unforgiving. But this winter was ten times worse.

The only thing Morgan could see was white. A sheet of unblemished and endless snow lay in front of her. Snow lifted off the surface and danced wildly in the air like ghosts. There was no sign yet of the forest Eli had drawn on the horizon. No sign anywhere of the village. No footprints that might lead her to him. Just white. Terrible white. It could have been that she was walking for minutes, or hours, but she carried on, kept peering through the storm to see something, anything. She carried on until her legs refused to go one more step, and the white slate in front of her began to turn black.

"Eli!" she cried desperately. "Eli!"

She'd wanted to save him, but needed saving herself.

The black came in tiny spots. Those spots grew in Morgan's vision. *Don't just die, Morgan. Do something*, she thought. She needed to shield herself from the wind and, somehow, the cold. The storm crushed her from all sides. There was only one place to go: down. She shoveled snow until her arms and hands and fingers wouldn't move any longer. She lay down in the hole she had made. There, she curled into a ball, shut her eyes, and blacked out, murmuring, "I'm sorry, Eli. I'm so sorry."

"Iskwésis."

It sounded like a voice, but Morgan couldn't be sure. She couldn't be sure that she was even still alive. It was a distant whisper, fighting through the screaming wind. She kept her eyes shut. Tried to collapse even further into herself. Her body was shaking, burning.

"Tansi, young one."

This time, it was unmistakable. Morgan forced her head to turn and worked even harder to open her eyes. They'd been frozen shut; tears to ice. She'd superglued her fingertips together once and needed to pry them apart, and opening her eyes now felt very much like that. But, gradually, the black gave way to white, and in the middle of that white stood a silhouette.

Morgan blinked to try and focus.

The figure leaned towards her, extended its arm, and when it did, flashes of a nightmare came into her mind. It was the fisher. He had black eyes, brown fur, rounded ears, a snout with a black nose and white whiskers. He wore clothing, too. A long-sleeved hooded jacket made of light-brown leather, beige pants, mukluks.

"Iskwésis, astum. Come with me."

When he opened his mouth, she saw something else about him: four long, sharp teeth.

"N-no," she forced out through trembling teeth and lips.

"Astum!" the fisher demanded.

What choice was there? Morgan took the animal being's paw, and he lifted her to her feet. Wrapping her arm around his shoulders, he put his own arm around her waist and urged her onward, but they'd gone only a few yards when she collapsed. Sank into the snow, almost as deep as when she'd dug a hole herself.

Morgan woke up staring at white again, and before long realized that she was being carried over the fisher's shoulders. She didn't protest. She stayed slack, as though still passed out, and just watched his legs dig into the snow, then lift out.

"How did you come here, Iskwésis?" he asked.

"Iskwé . . ." Morgan tried to repeat the word, but couldn't. Her jaws were frozen.

"Iskwésis," he repeated. "*Girl*. How did you come here?"

Morgan rubbed her jaws to give them some warmth and tried to speak again. "Through . . . a . . . draw . . . drawing."

She was too exhausted to consider how ridiculous it must have sounded.

"A drawing," the fisher said knowingly, as if it didn't sound ridiculous to him at all. "You came here through the Great Tree."

"That . . . big tree . . . yes."

"And why are you here?"

"Eli," was all she could say. Her jaw and mouth refused to comply any longer. Eli's name came out like a breath.

She wondered if the fisher had even heard her, but after a long time, he said, "The other one."

Morgan felt a burst of energy. She lifted her head, craned her neck, and stared right at the animal being. "You've . . . s-seen him?"

"Ehe," he said, "I've seen him."

"Wh-where? Where . . . is he?"

"Here."

They were entering a small village that consisted of longhouses constructed out of poles and bark cut into rectangular slabs, with rounded roofs of the same material. Each one looked about the size to fit one family, and they were built among pockets of particularly thick trees to provide shelter from the elements. There were seven in total, and the seven houses encircled a large thatched hut that stood in a perfectly round clearing. The hut was sheltered from the weather by the lodges and trees, and footprints led from the hut to each of the dwellings. There were firepits outside the houses, and racks that hung over the fires, used to smoke meat, but there weren't many pieces of meat hanging there. Scraps, if anything.

"Where is here?" Morgan asked.

The fisher lifted her off his shoulders with great care as they neared the entrance to one of the longhouses. She wobbled slightly. He steadied her.

"This is the only surviving village in the North Country," he said somberly. "Welcome to Misewa."

ELEVEN

"I . . . h-have . . . questions."

Morgan's knees felt like they were going to give out at any second. She was bracing herself against the long-house, standing near the front door. The village she'd just been introduced to was spinning into blackness. The fisher must have noticed. He had his paw firmly under her armpit for support, but it still didn't feel like enough.

"How is th-this even p-p-possible?" she asked. "Eli dr-drew this. It's n-not real."

The fisher laughed. "Iskwésis, the boy may have drawn Misewa, but it's very real."

"But how . . ." Morgan widened her eyes to keep them open, to fight off the darkness that was overtaking her vision. "How . . ." She was losing the fight.

"All things are connected," the fisher said. "Your world and this one, the sky and the land. All that is."

"So . . . you . . . know about h-humans?"

"Oh yes," he said, "I know about—"

Morgan's legs finally gave out. She started to fall, only to be caught by the fisher. He lifted her into his arms, and their eyes met. To her, his eyes were at once black, endless, and kind.

"Who are you?" she asked.

"I'm Ochek, and we need to get you into the warmth. There'll be time for questions later."

"Eli," Morgan whispered deliriously. "Eli."

Everything went black.

Morgan felt the sensation of being rocked. Slowly. Back and forth. She was being carried, but the howling wind and the cold were gone. In their place was warmth and the sound of a woman humming.

The song was familiar.

Morgan felt the same tug that she'd felt while standing in the snow, facing the Great Tree and the forest behind it. Drawn to the sound and the warmth and the rocking. She opened her eyes and was standing in a room with a lamp on a small table, a rocking chair, and nothing else except a window. Outside the window were ancient trees, thick and tall. Then there appeared a woman on the chair, and a toddler, a girl, in the woman's arms. The woman was rocking the sleeping child, humming a song to her. It was a sweet and gentle song, and the girl looked peaceful. But the mother was not peaceful. The mother was crying, trying not to sob. Sobbing might wake the girl.

"Kiskisitotaso," the woman whispered to the girl after the song had finished. "Kiskisitotaso."

A voice pulled Morgan away from the dream. Somebody was calling her name. She opened her eyes to find Eli sitting next to her.

"You're here." Morgan touched his face just to make sure it was actually him and she wasn't hallucinating.

"You're awake," he said.

Morgan propped herself up with her elbows. She felt stronger, and she was happy to be in the warmth. She was lying on a bed of spruce boughs, with a thick and heavy hide over her body. There was a small fire in a pit beside her bed casting light across the wooden walls. A chair sat unoccupied in the corner of the room, beside an opening that led to a room beyond. There was another empty bed of spruce boughs on the opposite side of the fire.

It was warm in the room, but the cold was still there, outside the longhouse. It announced itself with the wind, howling and pushing against the walls.

Morgan looked Eli over carefully. He wasn't in the clothes he'd been in earlier in the night. He was dressed like Ochek, wearing grayish pants, a brown jacket with a hood, and white moccasins. The only thing the same about Eli was his braided hair, neat and tight.

Braided hair.

The woman in her dream had had hair like that too. Hair like strands of midnight. Morgan pictured the woman sitting in the chair, rocking her baby. Singing to her. Whispering that word. *Kiskisitotaso.*

Morgan shook her head. "I was having a dream."

"No, this is real."

"That's not what I meant," she said. "I was *literally* having a dream, but it felt so real." Morgan focused on the woman and the word she'd repeated to the toddler. *Kiskisitotaso* It wasn't English. It was something else. Cree.

"Dreams can tell us important things," Eli said.

"Where you're from, your community, do they speak Cree?"

Morgan expected the smile to leave Eli's face at the mention of his home community, but it didn't. "Yes. Swampy Cree. It's a Cree dialect."

"Do *you* speak it?" she asked. "I mean, I know you know words and stuff. But are you, like, fluent?"

"Ehe." He nodded.

"The woman in my dream, she kept saying a word to a little girl. She was humming a song, and then she said one word over and over."

"What word was it?"

Morgan tried to say it properly, recited it deliberately. The sounds were hard and clumsy. "Kiss-kiss-it-ot-aso."

"Say it again, like you remember it," Eli said. "Like you can speak it. Like you've always spoken it."

"But I haven't. I never did."

"You know it, even if you don't think you do."

The boy who she'd known for a week seemed much older, and in only a matter of hours. *It is in his eyes,* she thought. Quiet and sure.

She took a breath, thought of the dream, of the woman and how the word came off her lips. "Kiskisitotaso."

"I know that word," he said. "In English, it means something like 'Don't forget about who you are' or 'Don't forget yourself.' That's pretty close."

"Why would I dream that word?" she asked. "Why would I dream that woman?"

"Sometimes you can dream a memory," he said.

"A memory," she repeated.

Morgan held on tight to the dream, even as it tried to pull away and leave only fragments. She held on tight to the woman's face. Morgan gasped, put her hands over her mouth, and a tear fell. "That was my mom."

"Morgan . . ." Eli reached forward and put a hand on her shoulder.

The shock of the realization, the longing she'd felt, left in a snap. In its place, all she could feel was anger. The burning in her chest boiled over and coursed through her body like blood. She pushed his hand off her shoulder and buried herself under the hide blanket.

"What were you thinking, going off like that, huh?" she said. "Did you even think about how I'd feel?"

"I did, it's just—"

"It's just what? You can't possibly have a good excuse for what you did. You could've died, and then what?" She pulled the blanket just low enough to see him.

"It reminded me so much of home when I saw Misewa for the first time." He stared into the fire. "I miss home so much."

"Dammit, Eli!" Morgan's breathing went from almost hyperventilating to calm in no time. She looked at him from under the security of the bedding. "I'm sorry for saying what I did. About pretending this was your home."

"I can hardly remember that." He grinned warmly at her. "Don't worry about it."

"I think I was jealous, you know? Because you can *remember* your memories," she said, "not just dream them."

"It doesn't matter," he said. "Not anymore."

"You know what's messed up?" Morgan got out of the hide blanket entirely, so that she and Eli were sitting across from each other. "That way you feel about here, I kind of felt in my dream. Even . . . I don't know . . . even now I know it was my mom. I mean, for all I know, that was the last time I saw her. Before she let me go." Morgan fought back tears. "If she didn't want me to *forget myself,* then maybe she should've kept me around."

"Maybe she should have. Maybe she didn't have a choice."

"Don't say that. You don't know that."

"Sorry."

"Anyway"—Morgan shook it off—"how can anybody remember who they are when they're never in the same place for more than a couple of years?" She felt the anger bubbling again, right inside her chest. Hot and quick. "She's just this stupid memory to me now and that's all! And so"—her shout fell to a whisper—"so is whoever she wanted me to be."

"Okay." He looked like he was going to cry. Tears were welling up in those huge eyes of his.

Morgan tried to steady her breathing. "I'm not angry at you. You're just *here,* that's all."

A long silence followed. All they could hear was the crackling of the fire and the gusting wind. During that time, they looked at each other, then away from each other, then all around the room. Morgan spent time assessing Eli's clothing, and how he had changed, and thought it was remarkable that he looked this way after such a short period of time.

How much time, exactly? She wished she hadn't left her phone in the bedroom.

"How long was I out?" she asked.

He thought about it for a moment. "An hour maybe?"

An hour. And the walk here had taken who-knew-how-long, because she'd passed out. Again. She was becoming the fainting queen. By now, it would be getting close to morning back on earth. On earth? Was this *not* earth? It couldn't be. Earth didn't have talking animals. Her fantasy-reading brain kicked in, leaving behind, for a moment, her worry about time. It couldn't be earth, but they couldn't be on another earth either, because they hadn't actually traveled anywhere. They'd just stepped through a portal, not flown somewhere on a spaceship. Maybe this was some kind of parallel dimension. Yes, that had to be it. She'd read about parallel dimensions. Oh! Morgan's heart skipped. It was like the multiverse in *Spider-Man*! And, like, lots of other comic books.

"Morgan," Eli said. "I said you'd been out for an hour? Hello?" He waved a hand in front of her face.

Okay. She took a breath or two. Now that the theory of the multiverse had been solved, she returned to her worry about time. Actual time. If it was close to morning, that meant they had to start going, like, now.

She stood up. "We have to get moving."

He sprung to his feet. "What? Where?"

"Home? Where do you think?" She moved for the door.

He stepped in her way. "No! Why?"

"Because Katie and James are going to be up soon and I don't want them to freak, that's why! Now move."

Morgan tried to push past him, but he didn't budge.

"It took you two weeks to come find me and all of a sudden you're worried about getting home before morning?"

"Wait, what? Two weeks? You've been here for two weeks?" Morgan held her head with both hands like she had the world's worst migraine. "Shut up! Why would you say that?"

"Say what?" he asked. "I'm just guessing. I don't have a calendar or a phone or anything. Ask Ochek, he—"

"*Weeks.*" She leaned towards him with deadly serious eyes.

"Give or take a day?"

"You're lying," she stated flatly.

"I don't know what you want me to say," he whispered.

"I left the secret room maybe a few hours ago, Eli. At most. *You* left the room *maybe* two hours before me."

"But—"

"This is . . ." She sat back down on the spruce boughs because she felt like she might faint again. "This is just . . ." Now it wasn't just a multiverse, but time too. Hours in her reality, weeks in this one. Was that why Eli looked so different? Was he telling the truth? How could that even be? "You have to be lying. You *have* to be."

"I'm afraid the boy's telling the truth." Ochek entered the room and sat down in the unoccupied chair. "It *has* been over two weeks since he arrived in Misewa. I've been making notches to count the days since—"

"Since what?" Morgan tried to keep her voice calm. Seeing Ochek for the first time when she wasn't delirious from the cold was very unsettling.

"To count the days since the White Time began," Ochek said.

"Show me," she said, which may as well have been her saying, *Prove it*. There was no way that Eli had been gone two weeks.

Ochek got up from the chair. "Follow me."

Morgan and Eli followed Ochek into a living area. It was a modest room with one shuttered window and furnished with two benches on either side of a firepit. Arranged on shelves were baskets holding what seemed to be dwindling amounts of preserved foods and medicines, and plates, cutlery, and cups that were all made out of bone and clay. Almost every inch of the wooden walls was marked with notches. One for each day. Countless notches. Ochek was near the front door, crouching in front of a small span of unblemished wood near the floor. Eli and Morgan knelt down on either side of him, just in time to see him make one more notch.

"See here?" He pointed to a mark.

"Yeah," Morgan said.

"This is when I saved Eli from the Barren Grounds, just like I saved you from them today." Ochek then methodically tapped each subsequent mark until stopping at the one he'd just made. "Today, right here."

All told, including the freshly cut notch, Morgan counted fifteen.

Two weeks and one day.

"This can't be happening," she said.

"Trust me." Ochek stuck the knife into the wall, and it stayed there in place. "It is."

TWELVE

Morgan, Eli, and Ochek sat on the benches in front of the firepit. Morgan was reaching her hands out towards the fire, taking in the warmth gratefully. Ochek and Eli hadn't stopped looking at her, waiting for her to say something about the truth she'd just learned: Eli had been living here for fifteen days. But she didn't know what to say, because she didn't know what to think, so she just stared into the crackling flames. At least she'd calmed down now. Not long ago, her heart had been pounding out of her chest like she was in some Looney Tunes show. Was it any different, though, that instead of a kids' cartoon, she was actually in a fantasy world? She'd always escaped, in a way, to the worlds she was reading about, but . . . to actually do it?

See here? She could hear Ochek clearly in her memory. *This is when I saved Eli from the Barren Grounds, just like I saved you from them today.*

She repeated his words over and over in her mind. In the

end, it was how he'd said the words, rather than what he'd said, that brought Morgan out of her silence.

"*It has been over two weeks since he arrived in Misewa,*" Morgan said in her best Ochek impression. "Shouldn't you have said something like, 'Eli has been here for many moons,' or something? You talk exactly how people talk. Humans."

"That's silly," Ochek said. "Who would talk like that? *Many moons.*" He scoffed. "The sun rises and falls and rises again. One day. Simple."

"That's seriously what you want to know, Morgan?" Eli asked.

"No, I just . . ." Morgan rubbed her temples. "I have a million things in my head and I have no idea how to get them out."

"Maybe I can try to answer a question you had when you first got here," Ochek offered.

"I really don't remember much about that," she said. "I passed out, if you'll recall?"

"You asked before how I would know about you," he said. "About humans."

She shrugged. "I mean, yeah. That was probably one of the million things I was wondering."

"Years ago," Ochek began, "a man came into this place. He arrived through the same portal that you did, in the Great Tree. Back then, the journey from the Great Tree to Misewa didn't seem as long. The Barren Grounds weren't so arduous. We were living in the Green Time, when birds and fish and four-legged animals were plentiful, and the land provided everything that we needed."

"See?" Morgan almost got up from the bench. "*That's*

what I'm talking about. The Green Time. *That's* fantasy-world talk."

"Why does she keep . . . ?" Ochek looked to Eli.

"Just keep going," Eli whispered to Ochek.

Ochek continued. "The man told us that he came in a good way, and we trusted him, took him into our village. He lived with us for a long time. He learned how to hunt and snare and forage, and we constructed an eighth lodge for him in which he lived. But there came a time when all that was provided to him, which is all anybody would need to live the good life, wasn't enough. He began to want more, and so took more. Of course, we noticed that our stores were getting lower and that the man began to change.

"You might think he would get full and content, consuming everything the way he was, but it was the opposite. He became gaunt and tired, and the more he took, the more he needed. He took so much that the game around the village began to dwindle. The birds and fish and four-legged animals weren't willing to provide for us anymore. Others in Misewa began to starve while the man got hungrier, and thinner, and we became afraid of him. Council, under the guidance of our Chief, Muskwa, decided to banish the man in order to save our village."

Ochek paused. Morgan, and even Eli, who had certainly heard this story before, waited. Tears had wet the fur under the animal being's eyes. They glistened like stars against a black sky.

"What's 'Muskwa' mean?" Morgan whispered to Eli as Ochek gathered himself.

"Bear," Eli whispered.

"Oh, so . . . their names are just what they are?"

"Not exactly."

"Not exactly? He literally calls me Girl. What does 'not exactly' mean?"

"Well, he calls *me* Eli, so . . ."

Ochek went on with a quivering voice that evened out only once the worst parts were told. The kids stopped their whispered conversation to pay him their full attention.

"On the morning he was to be sent back to his world, through the Great Tree, the village woke to a different world. The man was gone, along with one of our own. Tahtakiw."

"That means 'crane'," Eli whispered to Morgan.

"See?" Morgan whispered.

"Tahtakiw had been convinced by the man to run away and lead a different life," Ochek said.

"Why would Crane do that? Betray you like that?" Morgan asked.

"Maybe he knew what was coming, and didn't want to suffer, like we have suffered," Ochek said. "You see, the summer birds were gone. They were the ones who brought warmth to the North Country, which created the Green Time, which ensured the land had the means to provide for us. The wind was hard and strong, the grass and leaves were covered in snow, and the waters were frozen in place as though stuck in time. The weather wasn't new to us, but there had always been a cycle. The birds would travel across this place and distribute their warmth. The Green Time led to the Dying Season, which led to the White Time, which led to the Birthing Season. We set off after the man, but he had gone too far already and we couldn't find him. Misewa has lived through this cold ever since, and now we are dying."

Ochek put a paw on Eli's shoulder.

"Eli came here through the Great Tree. I was there to greet him."

"Why? How did you know?" Morgan asked.

"The answer to that is for a different time," Ochek said. "What's important now is that he greeted me in the good words."

"That's Cree," Eli said proudly.

"Still, I've kept him a secret to others, for my own reasons. I'll need to keep you a secret too, Iskwésis. But Eli here is able to live how we live. He is good on the land. I've taken him out with me on my trips, to check my snares and reset them, to forage for foods and medicines, to hunt. He eats only what is given to him. He respects this place and the beings within it. He is living here in a good way. He's been waiting for you, and because of that, so have I. It's why I was able to find you over the Barren Grounds, or else we might have been waiting forever."

Morgan's head was spinning. Fifteen days, in Misewa time. The North Country. Whatever Ochek called it. This place. In earth time, for Morgan, it had been maybe two hours, depending on when Eli had left while she was asleep. Math was never really her strong suit, but the calculation wasn't rocket science. Every week here was probably around an hour in earth time. That was a good thing. Because if she'd been here a few hours, it was probably a few seconds on earth.

"Well, we should probably go," Morgan said abruptly.

"What?" Eli looked as if his heart had been torn out of his chest. "Why? I don't want to go anywhere."

"You've been waiting for me?" Morgan asked. She wasn't sure she believed that. He'd come because it reminded him of home, not to lead Morgan here. "I came here looking for *you*, to bring you back. We can't just . . ." Morgan went for the door. She stared at the marks that indicated the days Eli had been here, and the knife sticking out of the wood. "We have to go. We can't just leave our earth and stay here. I promised Katie that I wouldn't run away. This would be running away. Like, super far away."

"*You* promised Katie," Eli said. "I didn't. What's there for me now? They're not my family. I got taken away from my family."

"Yeah, but Eli . . ." Morgan went back over and sat next to him. She put a hand on his shoulder. "Even if you're not with your family, they're still waiting for you."

"How long have you been gone from your home, Morgan? Do you think your mom is still waiting for you?"

Morgan felt as though she'd been punched in the stomach. "That's not fair. You know that's not fair and that it's totally different."

"I'm sorry," he said. "That was . . ."

"Very Morgan of you?"

"Yeah. You could put it that way."

"What's this about your mother, Iskwésis?" Ochek asked.

"Nothing," Morgan said. "It's nothing. I just have to go back before Katie and James wake up. That's all."

"Katie and James," Ochek said, "these are your parents? Are you children brother and sister?"

"They are *not* my parents," Morgan said. She tried to douse the flame in her chest with a few deep breaths. She spoke lower. "But Eli is kind of my brother, in a way. I'm responsible for him. That's why I walk him to school, walk him home from school."

"What is school?" Ochek asked.

"Well, at least you're acting like a fantasy creature," Morgan said. "School's where teachers make kids redo poetry assignments even when the first poem they wrote is really good."

"Poetry?" he said.

"I'll fill you in on the walk back to the Great Tree." Morgan got up again. "Eli, come on."

"Can't we just . . . ?" Eli stood beside her and looked up at her with those eyes of his. He may as well have been holding a black pirate hat against his chest, like that Puss in Boots GIF Morgan had seen a million times. "You said I was gone for, like, two hours and I've been here for two weeks, right? Can't we just stay here a bit longer, like a week, and still get back before Katie and James are awake?"

Morgan looked at Eli suspiciously. "I see you've done the math."

"It wasn't hard," he said.

"No, I guess it wasn't." Morgan went over to the shuttered window, stared through its cracks like there was something to see, but there wasn't. The snow seemed to overtake even the darkness. The White Time was the best name ever for the season this place was stuck in. "What is this place anyway? Like, the whole place."

"Askí," Ochek said.

"Earth," Eli whispered.

"Well"—Morgan turned away from the window—"the whole darn place should be called the Barren Grounds. What are we even going to do here for a week, Eli? Have snowball fights?"

"We're going to help," Eli said.

"Help?" Morgan said. "How can I help a village full of . . ." She looked at Ochek. "Are you all animals here? Walking, talking animals?"

"In the village or everywhere?" Ochek asked.

"In the village," she said.

"Then yes," he said.

"Okay," Morgan continued, "how can I help a village full of walking, talking animals stuck in some never-ending winter?"

"You can help like I've been helping," Eli said.

"Eli, I don't know the first thing about what you've been doing out here."

"We can teach you," he said.

Morgan threw her arms up in the air. "Have you even looked for this guy? The one who stole your birds or whatever?"

"We've no idea where the man went those many years ago," Ochek said. "Askí is big and our time is short."

"The Green Time is only where the man lives," Eli said. "Wherever the summer birds are, they're being held captive. It's winter *everywhere*."

"And I guess even if you went on a search party, you'd starve to death if you didn't find the summer birds, like, right away," Morgan said.

"We'd have to know exactly where to look, yes," Ochek said.

"Well, that sucks," she said, and nobody spoke for quite a long time. Then Morgan remembered the conversation that she and Eli were having before. "So, this man, just curious, I know he's evil and everything, but . . . what did you call him?"

Ochek looked ready to speak, stopped, then said, "Napéw."

Morgan wondered if that was what he'd originally intended to say. Regardless, she prompted, "And 'napéw' means . . ."

Eli sighed as he responded. "Man."

"Okay!" Morgan clapped her hands. "So, every being on Askí is literally named after what they are. Girl. Fisher. Man. Bear. For real?"

"Not always," Ochek said defensively.

Morgan continued as though Ochek hadn't said anything. "What if there are two of you in the same village. Like, two fishers. Is it like Dr. Seuss? Thing One and Thing Two? Or what?"

"What is Dr. Seuss?" Ochek asked.

"He was a writer. Never mind that," Morgan said.

"Well, I'm not going to name every being on Askí, if that's what you want," Ochek said.

"Just call them what they want you to call them, Morgan," Eli said through his teeth, chiding her.

"But Eli's Eli and I'm Girl," Morgan said. "Just to clarify."

"I've known him for weeks now," Ochek reasoned. "That's why."

"Seems a little sexist maybe, that's all," Morgan said under her breath, shrugging.

"Stay here with us. We could use your help," Ochek said.

"I don't want you to call me by my name *that* bad," Morgan said. But then she looked at Ochek, noticed how even he, who seemed so powerful, was thin. His clothes looked too big on him. At some point, they had probably fit him just right.

"I am the only hunter well enough to do the work. With you here, Iskwésis, we could survive longer," Ochek said.

"How much could I even learn in a week?" she asked.

"You learn by doing," Ochek said. "Being on the land is being with the best teacher."

Morgan took a deep breath. She looked at Eli and saw the hope in his eyes. And saw something else: happiness, even in the midst of this barren world. How could she take that away from him, when he was right? They could stay a week, go back, and nobody would be the wiser. She looked at Ochek. Proud. Strong. Dying. What if she *could* learn? Do the things that she'd never got the chance to do, because her mother had given her away when Morgan had been so young? What if she could do something, anything, to help them survive here, even for a bit longer? Finally, she looked at the knife stuck in the wall. It was primitive, not a calendar event she could enter into her phone, but it would tell them when they needed to leave.

Seven notches. Seven days.

"Fine," Morgan said. "We'll stay. We'll help."

"For real?" Eli beamed.

"Yeah, for real," she said.

"Ekosani," Ochek said. "Thank you. Southeast of here, through the forest, is my trapline. It's a difficult journey. We'll need strength and rest."

"I passed out twice, so I'm probably good," Morgan said. "Unintentionally well rested."

"Iskwésis," Ochek said, "the White Time is at its worst without the sun. It's best to wait until morning."

Morgan shuddered at the thought of the black this place offered, without any city lights, without even the flickering light from the fires at the longhouses. She'd already experienced it. What had she been thinking? She shuddered more than she would have from the cold.

"Okay, Thing One," she said. "Tomorrow it is."

THIRTEEN

The next day, Ochek woke the children up before the sun rose. For a moment, while Morgan's eyes were still closed, she thought she was in her bed. Her actual bed. And everything that had happened, from the moment they'd first discovered the portal to when she'd gone to sleep, was just a dream. A very elaborate, lifelike dream. She even reached out blindly and poked at the ground, trying to find the snooze button on her phone.

Morgan didn't know it was real until Ochek said, "Come, children, we have to leave before anybody else in the village gets up."

"Just a few more minutes," Morgan said, still half-asleep, with her mouth pressed against the hide blanket. "Please. Seven minutes is like one second in earth time, right?" She could still imagine she was home and that she actually had pressed the snooze button.

Weird, she thought, *imagining a real world instead of a fantasy one.*

"Sorry," Ochek said. "Your presence here needs to remain a secret, and to get where we need to go, leaving now is best."

"Great. Win-win."

"What does that mean? Two things can't win at the same time."

"She's being sarcastic." Eli was out of bed and looking like he'd already had a pot of strong coffee. "She doesn't really think it's great *or* a win-win."

"I almost froze to death last night so I'm tired," Morgan said. "Sue me."

"The point is, if Council found out I was keeping humans with me, I don't know what decision they'd make."

"Well, you catch all the food, don't you?" Morgan asked, finally pushing herself out of bed. "What are they going to do, banish you?"

Ochek shrugged, as though she had a good point.

"The last time they saw a human, he left them in eternal winter, Morgan," Eli said. "They probably won't like seeing us."

"I'm up. I'm up already," Morgan said.

They ate the same meal for breakfast as they had for dinner: dried meat and broth. Underwhelming, but as filling as one could expect in a village that was desperately hungry. Eating even the thumb-sized jerky they were given made Morgan feel guilty. She lamented that, in her haste to follow Eli, she had not packed a snack; if she had, she wouldn't have had to eat what little food Misewa had left.

Ochek prepared a pack for each of them to bring on their journey to his trapline, and soon after finishing breakfast, they set off through what felt like an abandoned village. If firelights had not been visible through the windows of the seven longhouses, you'd never have guessed there was anybody in Misewa but the three of them.

"What other walking, talking animals are here?" Morgan's fantasy-loving brain wanted to see all of them. She only knew, for sure, that there was Ochek and Muskwa.

"I've only ever seen Ochek," Eli said. "Every time I've gone out with Ochek, we've left just as early."

"I'm not that excited to see a huge walking bear," she admitted. "But, like, a turtle or something? *Awesome.* Maybe it'd look like a Teenage Mutant Ninja Turtle. Oh! What if its traditional name just happened to be Raphael or something?"

"At home, if we saw a bear, we would lay tobacco down, because bears mean healing," Eli said.

"That only makes them seem *slightly* less scary to me," she said.

"I was scared seeing them too," he admitted.

"Muskwa used to be feared in that way a long time ago," Ochek said. "Now he is a respected Elder and leader."

"How do you go from being one thing to another?" Morgan asked.

"He learned humility," Ochek replied, and left it at that.

Morgan had been afraid that the North Country might be stuck in a never-ending blizzard, with strong, freezing wind all the time and snow that felt like needles poking against her skin. She was relieved to find the weather pretty calm. There was wind, but it wasn't heavy. It was cold, but it wasn't biting. Morgan considered that this may have been because Ochek had given her clothing to wear that was a lot warmer than her hoodie. Still, the terrain was difficult. The trees were thick and the woods felt endless. The snow drifted even in the forest, which made it difficult to find footing. The wind had blown down trees, which forced the group to walk around them.

They headed southeast, and it was a long time before they stopped to rest. By the time they did, for lunch, Morgan was more tired than ever before. They found a spot to eat against a particularly large tree, and she felt like a rag doll collapsed at its trunk.

"How much longer?" she asked, like a kid in the backseat on a road trip.

"We should be there by nightfall," Ochek assured her, but all that meant was that they had another half day's journey ahead.

Their packs weren't all that big, but Morgan's was starting to feel like a boulder.

Ochek and Eli got to work making their lunch, and Morgan could tell they'd developed a routine. Although Morgan was tired, she helped as well, under the animal being's tutelage. As a group, they gathered kindling and wood, dug out a hollow in the snow, and built a fire. Eli looked proud in sparking the fire with stone (he exclaimed that it was the first time he'd been able to). She was shown how to make broth with melted snow and pine needles.

They ate the soup with dried meat.

The day wore on, the sun began to set, and the forest grew darker and colder. In the darkness, Morgan walked even closer to Ochek without really noticing. And whenever there was a sound that wasn't the wind, her head would jerk to attention. She would grab Ochek's arm, then quickly let go.

"Sorry," she would say each time.

Quite suddenly, they came to a canyon that cut right through the forest.

"I hate this part." Eli crept to the edge of the cliff and looked down.

Morgan could see why after she'd inched forward on her stomach . . . it had felt safer to do it that way. There was a frozen river at the bottom of the canyon that looked like a massive snake. Morgan estimated the river to be at least a hundred feet down. The canyon itself was twenty feet wide; on the other side, the forest started up again, as thick and wide as ever.

"Did you learn to fly over the last two weeks?" Morgan asked Eli.

Eli just nodded to where Ochek was expertly walking across the canyon on top of a felled tree.

"Oh," she said. "Fun."

"Come on." Eli followed Ochek across the canyon. He made his way more slowly than Ochek, but with good balance. Once there, he stood beside Ochek and looked to Morgan, who was still on her stomach. "Morgan!"

"Just give me a second!" Morgan pushed herself to her feet in slow motion. Her heart beat faster the closer she got to the tree bridge. She walked slowly, and stalled further when she got there by deciding to inspect how the tree had been cut down.

"That was Amisk's work!" Ochek said.

"That means 'beaver'!" Eli called over the expanse.

"Shut up, Eli!"

Morgan was busy with her thumping heart and shaking body, which wasn't shaking at all from the cold. The shaking wasn't helping her confidence in walking across the canyon. Looking at it now, the tree couldn't have been more than two feet wide. *I might as well be tightrope walking*, she thought.

"I can't do it!" she said.

"You've got great strength in you!" Ochek told her.

"This is a really bad time to talk like a fantasy character!" she said.

"It's either come here or go back on your own!" Eli said.

Morgan looked behind her, into the forest, and all she could see was night. No snow. No trees. Just a black hole ready to suck her up into oblivion. Heights or the dark. It was the balancing of fears. She turned back.

"Okay!" she said. "I'm coming across!"

She took a deep breath, swung her leg over the trunk, and pushed herself to her feet. She spread her arms out for balance and took a step forward, then another. At the very least, she was glad the weather was forgiving. She couldn't imagine doing this in the sort of wind she'd arrived in. Another step, followed by another. There may not have been wind, but the bark on the tree was slippery. For that, Morgan was glad Katie had given her moccasins. She could curl her toes around for some grip.

"You're almost there!" Eli said once she was halfway across.

Up until then, Morgan had kept her eyes trained on Eli the whole time and pretended that she was just walking along a fallen tree, not a fallen tree stretched over a profoundly deep canyon. That way, if she fell, it wouldn't be to crash onto a frozen river a hundred feet below, it would be more like dropping into a snowdrift. But, prompted by Eli's encouragement, she made the mistake of looking down. Everything began to spin like a kaleidoscope, and her foot slipped.

Morgan heard Ochek and Eli cry out.

She screamed as she toppled over and reached out in desperation. Both her arms managed to connect with the tree. Her fingers gripped the ridges of the bark, but with the leather mitts, she couldn't hold on.

"I'm coming!" Eli said.

Morgan watched him get back onto the tree bridge and make his way towards her.

He wouldn't get there in time.

Her arms and hands were sliding off, her fingertips unable to find a good hold. She let go with one hand and shook her mitt off, then quickly grabbed onto the tree again. She did the same with her other hand. As soon as her skin was exposed to the cold, her fingers started to go numb and stiff. It didn't matter that she could get a better grip.

"Hurry!" Morgan said.

"I'm trying!" Eli said.

Morgan tried to pull herself up, to force her fingers to work again, but her hands slipped off the bark.

"No!" Eli shouted.

Images flooded into Morgan's mind. The drawing. Ochek. Mrs. Edwards. Her poem. Their secret room. Finally, her mother. Rocking her back and forth.

Kiskisitotaso.

As she fell, Morgan reached out with one hand, and her fingers grabbed onto a frost crack. She dangled there, her legs and one arm free. She watched them as though they weren't a part of her body.

"Morgan, grab onto me!" Eli said.

She looked up to see Eli straddling the tree and extending his arm towards her. Her fingers were losing their hold. Her body was cold and tired. Every inch of it.

"I can't." Tears froze instantly against her cheeks.

"Yes, you can! I'm not going back without you."

Their eyes met, and he nodded at her.

"You can do it."

Morgan closed her eyes, gathered every bit of strength she had left, and thrust her arm through the air, towards Eli's outstretched hand. Just as her other hand lost its grip, she felt her hand connect with his forearm. He grabbed hold of her with his other hand, then grunted as he pulled her up. Once her stomach was firmly against the tree, she rotated her body and sat up straight. She didn't even care that she couldn't feel her hands, but Eli must have noticed them.

"Here." He took off his own mitts and handed them to her.

"Thank you." She slipped her hands into them. "What about you?"

"We can share."

Eli started to back away, towards an awaiting Ochek. Morgan slid forward on her butt, right behind him. When they got to the other side, she'd never felt happier to have her feet on solid ground and tried her best not to think about going over the worst bridge in history again on the way back to Misewa.

They all just stood there, looking at each other in a state of shock and relief, until Morgan said, "Please tell me we're almost there."

The group broke out into laughter.

"We're not almost there," Ochek said once they'd quieted. "We're here."

FOURTEEN

O chek's camp was a small clearing on the other side of the canyon, no bigger than ten feet by ten feet, and surrounded by forest. Trees weren't the only protection. The animal being had created his own snowdrifts, which encircled the camping area and kept a spot clear for the hut. They raised the dwelling, which was constructed out of thin poles and hide that Ochek had carried in his pack, and set up some spruce boughs and bedding inside, around a firepit. Again, Eli built the fire, and once this was all done, they sat around it together.

Morgan was thrilled to not only be alive, but to be in front of a fire and under a blanket. She was happy to stay there, warming her arms and hands at the flames and doing nothing else. Her fingers stung as they started to regain feeling, but it was a good sort of pain. Eli joined her there, warming his hands as well. Ochek waited until all the fingers in the hut were thawed out before getting a special treat ready for supper, a reward for such a difficult day.

"I've read about this at school," Morgan said with her mouth full. "Pemmican is like deer meat or something, all powdered up and mixed with fat."

"That's right," Ochek said. "Pimíhkán. Too bad there are no berries in it."

"It's so good," Morgan said. It tasted all kinds of amazing and was filling too. "I mean, maybe everything tastes good after almost dying, but it sure beats dried meat and broth."

"Don't get too excited," Ochek said. "Depending on what we find here, that might just be what we eat all the way back to Misewa."

"Isn't there a spot closer than this for hunting?" she asked after devouring the pimíhkán.

"There was." Ochek chewed at his own supper. "But as time has passed, the four-legged ones have either been caught or moved farther away."

"Do you think they found the Green Time?" Eli asked.

Ochek shook his head quickly at the idea. "They're just as weak as we are in Misewa. Even if they knew where the man went . . ."

"Could *you* find the man, if you knew?" Morgan asked. "If he was far away?"

"I'd have to," Ochek said.

"But you have to be as weak as the others," Eli said.

"Everybody has their role," Ochek said.

"Like what? Sitting around and doing nothing?" Morgan asked.

"There's more to do than hunt," Ochek said, and there was a long pause after this. Ochek, perhaps sensing that both Eli and Morgan wanted to know more, continued. "I was a child when Muskwa came into Misewa, and not much older than that when Council decided to make him Chief. Soon after he became Chief, the man entered our village. One of the first decisions Muskwa made was whether or not to accept the man into Misewa, and because . . ."

"Because . . . ?"

"He wasn't the first human to come to Misewa. The others were . . . good people. So, we thought, in our naivete, the man would be good as well."

"Are they still here? The others?" Morgan asked.

"They left many years ago," Ochek said.

"Where'd they go?" Eli asked.

"Back to your world," Ochek explained. "They came here in the same way as the man."

"Through the attic?" Morgan looked at Eli, puzzled.

"Maybe that's why it hasn't been opened for so long," Eli said.

"Eli, if somebody wanted to lock it shut, they'd use a *lock*, not a million layers of paint."

"Oh yeah. That's a good point."

"Exactly how many years ago?" Morgan asked Ochek, ready to do the math. "Like, how many notches or whatever?"

"Can I just . . ." Ochek threw his arms in the air. "I'm trying to tell you children a story. In good time, you'll find out about the others, alright?"

"Sorry," Eli said.

"Yeah," Morgan said. "Keep going. Sorry."

"The man came with what seemed like good intentions, so he was allowed to live among us. I didn't understand much back then. I was the youngest in the village. After the man left with the summer birds, with Tahtakiw, after the White Time fell on us, there were no other children born. Instead, over time, more and more of us died. We just couldn't have any more mouths to feed. So"—Ochek, who had been staring into the empty bowl, looked up—"I have remained the youngest and the strongest. Strong enough to be the one to hunt on the land and provide for the others. Strong enough to find the man, if I only knew where to go."

They needed rest before checking Ochek's traps. It had been a long, hard day, walking from Misewa. After Ochek finished his story, they settled in for the night. Morgan lay close to the fire, facing it. She closed her eyes but, despite her exhaustion, didn't fall asleep quickly. She listened to the wind outside, its distant hollow song serenading her as it danced through the trees. She listened to the fire crackle softly, like it was trying to be quiet, trying to allow them rest. Amid these sounds, her mind wandered.

She tried to think if this was the first time she'd ever been camping. She was sure it was. A family she'd stayed with a few years earlier—family number five, she guessed—had gone on camping trips, but hadn't taken her with them. They'd seen fit, just like the family before Katie and James, to send her off to respite instead. What was so awful about her that they'd rather leave her behind than take her with them?

And then she thought, *Am I awful?*

Yesterday she had been, she knew that much.

She pictured her mother in the tiny room. She imagined herself outside the room, looking at her through the window. No matter how hard she tried, she couldn't imagine herself *in* the room. She couldn't imagine herself in her mother's arms, being sung to, being told, in Cree, not to forget herself. But what was there to forget? That question, asked like a voice-over to the short film playing in her mind, of her mother in the room, and her outside in the cold, was the last thing Morgan remembered before finally falling asleep.

In the morning, they ate a quick meal (broth and dried meat again; no more pimíhkán) and took down the hut. The wind had returned overnight, and without three bodies weighing it down, the dwelling would certainly have flown off into the forest. Depending on how the day went, they'd either set it up again that night in the same spot or make camp somewhere on the trek back to Misewa.

The relentless wind and cold made the hours spent checking traps all the more frustrating. It felt like braving the elements should yield some kind of reward, even the smallest of animals to bring the villagers, but time and again they were met with the same reality: an empty trap.

"There've been many trips like this one," Ochek said at one point, seeing how disheartened the kids were, "and there've been trips that have been better."

"Some help we are," Morgan said to Eli. And then a thought occurred to her. "Did you catch anything when you were with him alone, just you two?"

"A couple of times," he said.

"You being here didn't keep the traps empty," Ochek assured Morgan.

Ochek had an empty sack over his shoulders, and it was

the saddest thing Morgan had ever seen. A knife was tucked into his belt to prepare the game on the spot. It would then be brought to Misewa to become clothing, utensils, and, most important, food. Morgan kept thinking about the racks she'd seen outside the lodges and how most of them were barren.

On they went, making their own tracks but finding no others and checking more traps with no animals in them. They had the smallest and least satisfying lunch behind a large tree that offered little protection from the wind and snow: broth made out of melted snow, pine needles, and bark.

After lunch, it was more of the same.

Morgan began to wonder if she should have come at all, if she shouldn't have just gone off with Eli from Misewa right when she'd found him.

"All I've done is start to care about them, and they're dying," Morgan said to Eli, quietly enough that Ochek couldn't hear. "What good is that?"

"I still wouldn't leave if I had a choice," he said.

"What?" She hit him on the chest. "If you stayed, you'd just die too. How does that make any sense?"

Morgan wasn't trying to be quiet anymore.

Eli looked at her with a stone face. "I'd be more alive here even if I was dying."

"Are you listening to yourself? You—"

"Shhh!" Ochek hissed at the two foster siblings.

They stopped fighting. Ochek was crouched down, staring off into the forest through the blustering snow. Without looking at them, without looking away from whatever he saw, he raised a finger and beckoned them over with it.

They eased forward with great care until they were at his side. He pointed in the direction he'd been staring.

"I don't see anything," Morgan whispered.

"Look." Eli pointed too.

She peered through the storm until she finally saw it. There was another animal being standing at one of the traps. It was oblivious to the group's presence.

"Maybe you're luckier than you think." Ochek pulled out his knife.

He started to move towards the animal. Morgan and Eli followed a safe distance behind, worried they would make a noise. It was a squirrel, maybe a foot shorter than Ochek and dressed in the same sort of clothing that he wore. Its bushy tail protruded from dark pants, and it wore a long-sleeved, green hooded top. The children didn't say anything to each other, just exchanged the same upset looks. How was it okay that Ochek planned to kill another animal being that walked on two legs? He'd talked about four-legged ones. Presumably, that's what the villagers in Misewa ate. Animals that didn't walk, or talk, and were the same size as the animals Eli and Morgan were familiar with in their world. This felt like a person killing a person.

When Ochek was nearly at the unsuspecting squirrel, with his knife raised and ready for the kill, Eli called out, "Run!"

The squirrel leaped to the side in time for the knife to stab into the trap, which was empty. The animal that had been in the trap, a hare, was now in the squirrel's mouth, and very dead, dangling half in and half out.

Ochek glared at Eli, and it sent a shiver down Morgan's spine. Eli backed away, and so did she.

"Isn't it one of your own?" Eli asked.

The squirrel spat out the hare and it landed on the ground, only somewhat chewed up. "Yes, aren't I?"

Ochek picked up the hare and stuffed it triumphantly into the once-empty sack.

"Let her go now," Morgan pleaded.

Ochek looked very much as though he wanted to get angry with the children, but instead he took a deep breath. "Children. Normally I'd agree, but we need this food."

"I am *not* food, thank you very much!" the squirrel said, appalled.

"Quiet, squirrel!" Ochek said.

"I have a name, *actually*!"

"You might as well eat *us*!" Eli said.

"Don't give him any ideas!" Morgan slapped Eli on the arm.

"Ow! Stop hitting me!"

"That's not the same," Ochek said. "I'm only trying to do what's best for my village . . ." As he continued to explain his position, the squirrel, in full view of both Eli and Morgan, began to sidestep away, very quietly. The foster siblings said nothing, hoping the squirrel could get far enough that when Ochek noticed, it would be too late. He was going on about the history of the village: ". . . understand that things will never be the same as before, when each season gave way to the next. We have to do what we can to survive. We honor each animal, two-legged or four, that gives of themselves for us."

"They'd probably prefer not to, though," Morgan grumbled.

Ochek started to turn towards the squirrel, who was now a good ten feet from them.

Morgan reached out and grabbed his shoulder. "Hey, can you tell me about . . . what Council would think of this?"

Ochek looked at her curiously, but answered. "If Council told me not to kill her, I wouldn't. Their rules govern Misewa, and we trust in those rules."

"But you were just about to kill her without Council telling you that you could," Morgan said. "How does that make sense?"

"It was impulse," Ochek admitted. "In the end, Eli may have been right to stop me."

"Because if she was dead and Council told you not to kill her . . ."

"Yes, I know," Ochek said. "I already conceded your point, Iskwésis."

"And another thing . . ." She crossed her arms for effect and tried to think of an actual other thing. While she did, she glanced at the squirrel. She'd not intended to. It gave her stalling tactic away.

"Clever girl!" Ochek wheeled around to find the squirrel still very slowly trying to escape. When the squirrel locked eyes with Ochek, she froze for a moment, and so did he. Then, like a bullet, he took off after her. She bounded away from him, and it was difficult to tell who was faster. The deep snow didn't impede either of the animal beings, and all Morgan and Eli could do was keep them in sight as they chased behind.

Ochek and the squirrel were quickly no more than specks against the tree-littered horizon, kicking up clouds of white flakes like a snowblower. Never mind the two animal beings, Morgan could hardly keep up with Eli. The best she could do was follow in the trail he was making, but even still, her legs started to burn from the pursuit. Finally, after either several minutes or forever, the animal beings stopped in an explosion of snow.

The squirrel was standing on the branch of a tree, just out of reach of Ochek, who was on the ground directly below the branch, knife at the ready. Even though the squirrel was agile, she couldn't run along branches and jump from tree to tree, since she was two-legged and much larger than a normal squirrel. So, she was safely out of reach, but stuck in place.

"You can't stay up there forever," Ochek warned.

"That's true," the squirrel said. "But I've just had a bit of a meal and should be okay for a little while."

"So should I," Ochek said.

"Can't we just check the other traps for food?" Eli asked.

"You're only delaying the inevitable," Ochek said to the squirrel, ignoring Eli altogether.

"If I'm going to die," the squirrel said, sitting on the branch, "I might as well enjoy the view." Ochek jumped and tried to grab her dangling feet, but missed.

"The view?" Ochek said. "We're in the forest, Arikwachas."

"Oh, *now* you're using my name, Ochek?" she chided.

"It's not that I don't respect you," Ochek said. "You're a . . . victim of circumstance."

"Well, if it's all the same, I'd like for you to call me Arik." The squirrel raised her chin and crossed her arms. "*If* you respect me so much."

"I can't say that you respect *me*, stealing from my traps." Ochek tried to grab Arik's feet again, but failed.

"I didn't see your name on them."

"You know they're mine!"

"Can I ask a question, even if you're both super worked up?" Morgan asked.

"*I'm* not worked up; he is," Arik said.

"Do you blame me?!" Ochek said.

"So this has to do with the traps and the hare you had in your mouth, Arik. Why is this even a thing? I mean, I thought squirrels just ate nuts and seeds and stuff like that," Morgan said.

"I'll have you know," Arik said, "that when food is scarce, like it has been for many years, squirrels like yours truly here will eat meat. That is, if they're smart enough to catch it." She looked down at Ochek with a smirk. "Or know where to find it."

"You stupid little squirrel!" Ochek, in his anger, missed Arik by a mile this time around, jumping and reaching wildly.

Arik laughed at the attempt, then sighed. "The sunset is pretty this time of year. I think I can hang on until then at least."

"You just go ahead and hang on. Two can play at that game." Ochek cleared snow away from the base of the tree, busily and angrily making a place where he could wait Arik out while being shielded, as much as possible, from the wind. "I can sit on the ground longer than you can sit in a tree," he grumbled, sitting down in the make-shift clearing with his back against the trunk and sticking his knife into the wood. The children joined him. Ochek looked sour. His arms were crossed, eyebrows furrowed, and he had an exaggerated frown on his furry, snow-freckled face.

"Are you pouting?" Morgan asked.

"No," Ochek snapped.

"You're *totally* pouting."

"I am totally *not* pouting."

While all this went on, Arik lay down on the branch and put her arms under her head. She looked, in the midst of the storm, as if she was relaxing in a hammock on a warm summer day.

"I could get used to this," she said.

"I'm just mad at you both, that's all," Ochek said to Eli and Morgan.

"*We* didn't run away from you," Morgan said.

"We just don't want you to eat something that walks and talks," Eli said.

"You've been here two weeks." Ochek, for the first time, sounded tired. "You'd think differently after decades of the White Time."

"I would *not*," Morgan said.

"Creator gifted some of us beings with the good words, and left many without them. Those creatures have always provided for us, and we honor them for it. They've left the area, and we are dying. I'll do anything to help Misewa survive," Ochek said.

"You know"—Arik turned on her side, still relaxed as could be—"I've been thinking. Let's say the White Time ended. Would you still want to eat me up?"

"What's the point of answering that question?" Ochek was growing more sullen by the moment.

"If I'm going to die at some point when I get off this branch, then why don't you humor me?"

"Fine." Ochek got to his feet. "If the White Time ended, no, I would not eat you." He scanned the area as though things really were different, as though—instead of snow and wind and cold—there was lush green grass and leaves, warm air, rushing water, and plenty of game. "The land would provide everything we'd need."

"I have a follow-up question," Arik said.

"Don't push it," Ochek warned.

"Just one more, I promise." Arik sat on the branch again, her legs kicking back and forth playfully. "Let's say that I knew where the summer birds were being held. Would you make a deal with me? Say, let me go in exchange for that information?"

"Liar!" Ochek leaped into the air and grabbed at Arik, but missed for a fourth time.

"I mean, I could be lying, but . . ."—she put a finger on her chin and stroked the fur—"what if I'm not? Are you willing to risk it?"

"If you knew where the summer birds are, where the man is, you would've gone there yourself!" Ochek said.

"Not really," she said.

"Yes, really," he said.

"Maybe I've been waiting for exactly the right moment," she said.

"And how many have died while you waited, if what you say is true?" he asked.

"Maybe this moment is the only moment that would ever have worked, dear friend," she said.

"I'm not your friend, and how would you know that?" he said.

"After all," she said, "it's very far and I have short legs. If you believe nothing else, you *have* to believe that. Plus, little ol' me against that big human?"

"Why should I believe anything you say, thief?"

"For the same reason, dear Ochek, that I would trust you and come down from this branch. What other choice do we have?"

Ochek looked at the children, who had remained sitting and watching the exchange with great interest. He looked at Arik thoughtfully. "Your deal is that you tell me, and I let you go?"

"In a nutshell," she said. "See what I did there? Nuts, squirrel . . ."

"I want to amend the deal," he said. "You tell me, I let you live, but you come with us to where the summer birds are."

"*Us?*" Morgan wondered how many days that would take, and how many hours on earth. The most they could be away was maybe a week and a half, and that was very loose math. Hopeful math. The kind she did for quizzes after forgetting to study.

"We have to help them," Eli said to her. "Please?"

"How far is it?" Morgan asked Arik.

"It's far, but not, you know, *far* far," Arik said.

"Like in miles," Morgan said.

"What's 'miles'?" Arik asked.

"Like compared to from Misewa to here?" Morgan said.

"Let's see." Arik scratched her temple. "It's like—"

"Arik!" Ochek said. "Do we have a deal?"

"I want to amend your amendment," Arik said with full-on squirrelly duck lips.

Ochek looked as if he wanted to pull his fur off. *"What now?"*

"If I'm to come with you," Arik said, "I think it's best I lead you there and not tell you anything at all right away. Male animals and directions, am I right?"

"No!" Ochek shook his head violently. "No deal! You tell me now, or that's that."

"Then kill me," she said. "You'll be full for a short while, but you'll have to come here again and again and again until forever has gone by and we'll all have died from starvation."

Ochek sighed heavily. "I don't know."

"Ochek," she said, "don't you think I want the Green Time back? Do you think it's fun for me to steal your food, to live like this, in the forever white?"

Ochek stuck his knife into his belt. "Fine, Arik. But if you're lying, I *will* serve you to the village for a feast, and gladly."

Arik jumped off the branch and extended her paw, looking pleased and relieved at the same time.

"Splendid!" she said. "We have a deal, then?"

"Nothing is done without Council's approval," he said.

"Oh, good," she said. "I've heard Misewa is lovely this time of year."

FIFTEEN

T he new group of four left immediately for Misewa, with
only a chewed-on hare to show for their trip. That, and
guarded hope. Morgan's heart felt like exploding when
they got back to the canyon, but she managed to crawl
across the tree bridge on all fours without looking down.
Once safely across, they carried on until it became too dark
and cold to continue, and they set up camp for the night. In
the hut, the children slept, Morgan more easily on her second night in the dwelling, and so did Arik. But Ochek stayed
up to watch the squirrel and make sure she didn't run off.

When morning came, they ate breakfast, divvying up the
hare among the four of them (Arik was given the smallest
portion because she'd already eaten some of it). They actually cooked it too, and this was a better treat than the
pimíhkán.

By afternoon the next day, their third day on Askí by
Morgan's count, they arrived in Misewa. Eli, Morgan, and
Arik were made to wait in Ochek's lodge while he asked to

see Council. The children were to keep the squirrel from leaving—Eli had been given Ochek's knife—and they dutifully stood by the entrance, blocking the way out. Arik, though, didn't seem as though she wanted to leave at all. She was cozied up by the fire looking positively happy.

"Why don't you live here?" Morgan decided that if they had to wait, they might as well talk.

"I kind of like to keep to myself," Arik said.

"But wouldn't it be easier to be in a community? A family?" Eli asked.

"The thing with that is," she said, "when you're a smaller two-legged pisiskiw, and everybody's hungry because of the White Time, it becomes a bit like survival of the biggest . . . and fittest. I'm fit, not big."

"Pisiskiw?" Morgan said.

"Animal," Eli explained.

Morgan and Eli, content that there was no threat of an escape, moved to the fire and sat across from Arik.

"What about before the White Time?" Morgan asked.

Arik nodded. "That was a very long time ago, but yes, I was in a community. Once they got their forks and knives out, I left."

"That's so sad," Eli said. "I don't know if I even want to meet the other animals here."

"Well, apparently they won't be too thrilled to meet us either," Morgan said.

"It's not so bad," Arik said. "I like living on the land, and I'm small enough to find big holes in even bigger trees that I can sleep in."

"You're, like, almost five feet tall!" Morgan said.

"Only on my driver's license," Arik said.

"How would you know about drivers' licenses?" Eli asked.

"Oh, right, sorry," she said. "Previous encounters with humans. And about the height thing, there are some pretty big trees in the North Country."

"You've got to be lonely, though, being out there like that," Morgan said.

"Fewer mouths to feed," Arik said. "One, to be exact. The great Misewa hunter sets his traps, but the joke's on him." She sighed. "He just makes it easier for little ones like me to find a nice supper!"

"You don't really like it on your own," Morgan said. "You can't."

"That's why you didn't keep running," Eli said.

"That's why you told Ochek about the summer birds," Morgan said.

"There's less and less food in the traps—less for them *and* less for me," Arik explained. "And I do feel bad stealing from others. Anyway, I'm glad you two showed up when you did. I could never have made the Green Time return on my own. Not against that human." Her shoulders slumped. "Plus, I thought that . . ."

"You thought what?" Morgan said.

"That maybe if I did well, they'd let me live *here*," Arik said very quickly, as though she was afraid the idea was silly. "If, you know, they wouldn't have to eat me."

"Were you trying to get caught?" Eli asked.

"At first, I was trying to get breakfast," Arik said with a laugh. "I thought of the other thing while Ochek was chasing me, and especially when I saw you children."

"Why us?" Morgan asked.

Arik shook her head and seemed to scold herself. "All I'm trying to say is that you have to think quickly in times like that. Two humans against one human, well, isn't that better than a bunch of animals all on our own?"

"I never said we would go," Morgan pointed out.

"What?" Eli said.

"Because you never told me how long this would even take!" Morgan said.

"Right," Arik said. "Well, I was kind of preoccupied with bartering for my life and all. Forgive me."

"We *have* to go," Eli said. "You heard her. Two humans against one."

"Two *kids* against a *man*," Morgan corrected Eli, then turned back to Arik. "First things first: do we even have time to help? We can be here for a week."

Arik rolled her eyes dramatically. "I mean, all the variables, children. It could be this, it could be that. How could one possibly know?"

"I need to know!" Morgan said. "Or I'm going to take Eli and we're going to go back to our world. Like, tonight."

"Alright, alright," Arik said. "Calm down now. Let me think." She closed her eyes tightly. "I'd say, to give you a range, four to seven days. But on the low end. Most probably four."

"We can still do it," Eli announced.

"Time-wise, yeah," Morgan said, "but if something happens to you, or us, and we just . . . disappear . . . then what? What do Katie and James do?"

"They need us to bring back the summer birds," Eli said. "They have to come back or else Misewa will die."

"I don't know."

Morgan stared at the notches of wood. Three days had gone by. Ochek had made three more marks before leaving them. They had a week left. But what if they were here longer, even for a day? Two? Would that be minutes on earth? Could they just say that they'd hidden in the attic, lost track of time? What was the worst that could happen? They'd get grounded?

The fire cast light and shadows against the marked-up walls, and in those shapes, like black clouds against an orange sky, Morgan saw the dream again. Her mother, sitting in a chair, rocking Morgan as a toddler. She heard the wind outside, and in the wind, her mother's song, and the word: *kiskisitotaso*.

She felt a pull. Not from her world, but here.

"Okay, we'll help," she said.

At that moment, the door opened and a gust of cold wind announced Ochek's presence. He looked all business.

"They'll see us now."

At once, Arik, Eli, and Morgan stood up to go, but Ochek held up a paw and cautioned the humans in the party. "I've explained to Council who you are and how you came here, and they weren't exactly happy about it. Say nothing unless you're asked to speak."

"*I* can talk, though, right?" Arik said. "Because I have a lot to—"

"Yes, you can talk," Ochek said, interrupting her. "Just . . . not too much."

They found the thatched hut in the middle of the village encircled not only by the seven lodges but by the occupants of Misewa. They were standing outside their homes, facing the humans and Arik and Ochek, all in various stages of shock and disbelief. Two foxes shared a wide-eyed look. A beaver slapped its tail at the sight of Eli and Morgan. A large, albeit frail, elderly bison sat on a log outside of its longhouse, shaking its head. A couple of moose just stared at the two humans, their mouths agape. An old muskrat with a thick hide wrapped over its shoulders looked to the left and right, at all its fellow villagers, searching for answers. And finally, a caribou threw a snowball at the kids, which hit Morgan, and yelled at them to leave. "Awas!"

"Keep walking," Ochek said.

"What's their problem with us?" Morgan wiped the snow away from her clothing.

"We're not like that other human," Eli said.

"I know that, children," Ochek said.

"At least they're not licking their lips at the sight of me," Arik said. "That's a bonus."

Council was waiting for them. There was a firepit in the middle of the hut, burning hot and bright. This was surrounded by large and smooth white stones. Beside the firepit was a small collection of medicines and dried, ancient-looking berries. Morgan thought that these were probably very precious, as nothing more would grow until the Green Time returned. The fire illuminated drawings all over the interior walls of the hut. At the head of the hut, in a northerly direction, was Council.

Council was made up of three beings: an owl, a bear, and a turtle. The bear, whom Ochek had called Muskwa, sat between the others. Though old, with gray speckled within its dark brown fur, it towered over the two Council members and the guests. It had forest-green pants that covered short, thick legs, and a black, tattered vest. What was most pronounced about the bear was a large scar across its chest; the pink skin glowed with the fire's generous light. To Muskwa's right was the owl, and unlike the other beings in the village, the owl looked mostly unchanged from any other owl Morgan had seen. That is, other than it wearing a cowl and holding a rickety walking stick in its feather-like fingers. Finally, to Muskwa's left was the turtle. It wore a cardigan made of dead grass over its shoulders, and its underbelly was painted in ocher with characters Morgan was sure meant something important. The turtle looked old and frail underneath its clothing, but its eyes were powerful.

"Api," Muskwa said with a thick and resonant voice.

Arik, Ochek, and Eli sat down. Morgan stood there, feeling awkward, until she figured out what "api" meant and sat down as well.

"Muskwa," Ochek said, "before we start, can I ask that we speak in the other words? This human"—he pointed at Morgan—"doesn't speak."

"But the other does," said the turtle, who sounded female.

"Yes, Miskinahk," Ochek said. "The small one does."

Muskwa looked reluctant, but let out a heavy breath, which the foster siblings felt from across the fire, through the warmth of the fire itself. "Very well."

The start of the meeting was familiar to Morgan. She remembered it from Orange Shirt Day at school. The great bear took out a smudge bowl and pinched some sage from the medicines beside the fire. He lit the sage with a twig at the edge of the fire, and a small flame erupted from the medicine. When the fire went out, smoke danced from the bowl towards the ceiling. He held it to his left, and Miskinahk, the turtle, fanned the smoke over her body, directing it over her eyes, mouth, heart, and torso. The smudging continued this way in a clockwise fashion, one being—animal or human—holding the bowl for the next, until the owl held the bowl for Muskwa, and he welcomed the smoke over his enormous body. The bowl was then placed in front of the bear and left there. Throughout their time within the hut, the smoke slowly died off.

"Oho," Muskwa said to the owl after the smudging had ended. "Would you lead us in prayer?"

"Ehe, Muskwa," the owl said, closing its eyes. Morgan thought the owl sounded neither female nor male.

"Creator," Oho said. "We ask that you be with us here, and help us to speak with each other in a good way. Grant us wisdom and a direction that will help the pisiskowak who live in this place. Ekosani."

"Ekosani," each being in the hut repeated, even Morgan.

Oho was the last to open their eyes. When they did, they were piercing and directed squarely at the children. "*Who are you?*"

The foster siblings introduced themselves, while Oho nodded slowly.

"Why did you bring them to Misewa?" Miskinahk asked Ochek.

"I didn't bring them here," Ochek said. "They came through the Great Tree on their own."

"And they walked through the Barren Grounds *on their own?*" Miskinahk asked.

"Okay, well . . ." Ochek squirmed. "Technically I brought them here, but, Muskwa, they would have died otherwise."

"*Who* do you wish to protect?" Oho asked. "This village or these humans?"

"Do you really have to ask that, with everything we've been through, Oho?" Ochek asked.

"Years ago," Miskinahk said, "Napéw came through the Great Tree after . . . others had come to this place. He followed them through, didn't he?"

"The point is—" Ochek started, looking ready to get up.

"The point is that you've endangered this village!" Muskwa said with a towering voice, and the room was brought to silence. "Others may follow these little ones, and you know very well that's true. Lives have been lost through sickness and hunger. And the good life . . ." The bear's voice cracked, and he paused. "We only have these walls to remind us of it."

"Man takes," Miskinahk said. "It is all he knows to do."

"Well, I'm not a *man*, in case you haven't noticed." Morgan stood, and she took a step towards the fire. "I'm a girl."

"Morgan!" Eli hissed under his breath. "Ochek said not to talk unless—"

"I don't need to just sit here and let them decide what kind of people we are!"

"But we *do* have to let them decide what we should do!" he shout-whispered. "Why do you always do this?"

"Do what? Stick up for myself?!"

"Iskwésis, you must—"

"Enough!" Muskwa said, interrupting Ochek.

The fire seemed to shout its crackling and snapping in the silence that followed. Even the wind was hushed.

"The girl is right," Muskwa said. "The actions of one don't predict the actions of another, and we need to be able to forgive what's been done in the past either way. I should know that more than most." He paused thoughtfully. "Why are you here, little humans?"

"To help, Muskwa," Eli said, following the don't-speak-unless-spoken-to rule. "In any way that we can."

Morgan, who'd been breathing deeply to calm herself, said, "Eli's right. We were going to go, but now I feel like we have to stay."

"Maybe," Eli said, "we can help give back what was taken from you."

"Maybe you can," Muskwa said.

"I know them to be good people." Ochek looked to the children, then to Arik. "They stopped me from killing this one, and now we might really have a chance to release the summer birds."

"And bring back the Green Time," Miskinahk said.

"What about you?" Oho looked straight at Arik. "Are we supposed to trust in you as well?"

Arik, who had been silent the entire time, cleared her throat. "I did tell Ochek here that he could kill me at any time if he found me to be untruthful. Bring me back, serve me for supper. I'd last at least a week. I'm sure that I'm very yummy." She nodded proudly at Ochek. "He's a very good trapper, I mean. Keeps me fed out there on the land. His traps, that is. I guess it's odd I'm asking you to trust me when I've been stealing your food, but in the balance of thieves, the man is *way* worse than me, and—"

"I think what she's trying to say, Muskwa"—Ochek shot Arik a steely glare—"is that she's putting her life on the line for this."

"I suppose we all are, in a sense, aren't we?" Muskwa asked. "By letting you leave, Ochek, we are letting go of our provider."

"*Who* says we'll survive the time he's gone?" Oho asked.

"Who says we'll survive much longer whether he leaves or not?" Miskinahk asked.

Muskwa stood up, and Council did the same. He walked around the fire on his own.

"You've always done what's right for Misewa," he said to Ochek, who bowed his head in response. "We've been waiting for death to find us. Perhaps it's time we found life."

SIXTEEN

Ochek, Arik, Morgan, and Eli left without much more than they'd had with them on their journey to Ochek's trapline. Their packs were filled with materials for their dwelling, eating utensils, extra clothing (something that would have been useful when Morgan had lost her mitts), food, a small shovel, and so on. Muskwa had asked them to take more rations than strictly necessary, in case Arik was wrong and they found themselves stuck deep in the White Time with a long way to come back and no food to sustain them.

Ochek refused to put the village at greater risk. "I haven't hunted in this direction for years," he said to Muskwa, "and so there might be more game."

One condition that Ochek had agreed to, at Arik's request, was that if they came across game, it would be of the four-legged variety.

"If they talk, they walk," she'd said. "I mean, they walk, like, they get to leave. Get it?"

"Yes," he'd replied. "I understand."

They headed south, as they had previously, but southwest rather than southeast. It made Morgan wonder if the villagers had ever gone north, across the Barren Grounds, to hunt. There were woods there too. If there were woods, there might be game. Even if, as on her world, it got colder the farther north you went. Besides, they all had fur, didn't they? But she decided questions about that would have to wait for another time. The weather was cruel again, and having a conversation while walking through it wasn't going to do any good.

For the better part of two days, Morgan couldn't see what was different in this direction to keep beings from Misewa away from it for so long. Years, Ochek had said. The trees were thick and tall. The snow was deep and soft and undisturbed; there were no tracks. It wasn't until the wind started to blow more aggressively on the second day that something began to feel different. It rudely elbowed through the oak and pine trees and caused snow to drift higher than any one of them thought possible, as high as a house back in the city. This, in turn, required the group to take long detours. Morgan realized that the trees were beginning to thin out, and the fewer trees there were, the harder the wind blew and the higher the snow drifted.

When they came to the end of the forest, Morgan finally understood why it was that no one came this way any longer.

A long and wide field stretched out in front of them, at least as imposing as the Barren Grounds. And in the distance, a mountain range stretched as far south and north as you could see. The highest peaks reached to the heavens, and even the lowest points looked hard to climb. The mountains looked like a line of sharp and crooked teeth, as if anyone who tried to cross might get eaten alive. They huddled together at the edge of the forest to shield themselves from the wind, with the great field in front of them and the mountains beyond. By this time, the sun was setting, light giving way to dark.

"We can't stop here," Ochek shouted over the wind He slipped his pack off, took out pieces of dried meat, and handed one to each of the group. "We have to keep going until we reach the base of the mountains. At least there we'll have shelter."

"Too bad," Arik said. "This is a wonderful place for a picnic."

"I can see why you didn't go on your own," Morgan said to Arik.

"Are you kidding?" Arik said. "It's stupid to go with four, never mind one." She stuck the meat in her mouth and started walking through the field. "But if we don't start moving, we'll become our own little mountain range!"

She was right. In the few minutes they'd been standing there, the snow had already started to creep up higher around their bodies. If they stayed where they were, they'd be swallowed up by one of the snowdrifts.

"You're sure this is the way?" Ochek called out to her. Even the great hunter sounded hesitant about what lay ahead.

"I should hope so, shouldn't I!" she called back.

It felt as if hours had gone by when Ochek stopped. By now, it was night, the sky was clear, and the stars and moon painted the snow in a shade of light blue. Morgan, who'd been trailing behind, taking advantage of the path the other three had cut through the snow, arrived last.

"Oh, crap," she said when she saw what had stopped Ochek.

It was the same canyon they'd crossed before, but this time there wasn't a felled tree to help them across. It was far worse. A narrow bridge of ice lay in front of them, frosted with snow at the edges but like glass down the middle. A gust of wind, a wrong step, and Morgan pictured herself slipping and falling. She got on her hands and knees, crept to the foot of the bridge, and slid her hands over its surface. It was very slippery.

"How did this even get here?" she asked. "Like, a literal ice bridge? Really?"

In the books she read, it would exist only because of magic, but while there were talking animals on Askí, she was pretty sure there were no ice queens sleighing around, manifesting Turkish delights to tempt little boys.

"I'm not sure," Ochek said. "It has been here since the arrival of the White Time."

"Pardon me. I usually love a good mystery but it's getting colder." Arik walked to the foot of the bridge. She turned to the group with a smirk, then got on all fours. "See you on the other side!" Just like that, she sprinted across the bridge like an actual squirrel and made it to the other side before anybody else could take a breath.

"*You* should be especially careful," Ochek said to Morgan before he, too, went on all fours and scampered across with little trouble, only a bit more slowly and less gracefully than Arik.

"Thanks for the tip!" Morgan shouted over the wind. She inched forward again, until she could hang her legs over the edge of the canyon, on either side of the bridge. She pressed both hands against the surface and was about to shimmy onto the ice, but she stopped and looked up at Eli. "Nobody would blame us if we just turned around and decided to, like, *live*, you know."

"We can't just leave them," he said. "You know we can't."

Morgan looked at the two animal beings, standing at the other side of the canyon and watching them intently. They seemed to care for the humans, and Morgan had to admit to herself that she was starting to care for them as well.

"You're right," she said. "Plus, I'm not sure I could find my way back, and Ochek has all the food anyway."

She let Eli go first again. He went the way Morgan intended to go: on his butt, straddling the ice, and pulling himself forward, bit by bit. Morgan did the same, right behind him, concentrating on the back of his head and not looking down. *There is no canyon, there is no canyon, there is no canyon*, she thought, all the way across. When she got to the other side, she let out a huge breath she hadn't realized she'd been holding.

Nobody paused to celebrate.

They kept on. The foot of the mountains was close, and the travelers were weary. Thankfully, even now the wind was softer, the snow wasn't as deep, and it turned out to be the easiest part of their journey. That is, until Ochek and Arik knelt down up ahead. They seemed to be involved in some sort of conference, which made Morgan feel very curious. When she and Eli caught up to them, the two animal beings were inspecting a set of animal tracks.

Morgan bent down and looked at the prints herself. She was no tracker, but she knew enough to tell that they weren't left there by a two-legged being. "They look like they're from a dog or something."

Eli looked at them as well. "No, they're from a wolf, right, Ochek?"

"Ehe," Ochek confirmed. "They're from a wolf."

"I'm sorry?" Morgan said.

"A wolf," Eli said.

"No, I heard him," she said. "I just feel like peeing my pants."

"Oh my," Arik said. "Your legs would get so cold."

"It was a figure of speech," Morgan explained.

"So you're not going to—"

"No, she's scared," Eli said. "So am I."

"Then I, too, may pee my pants," Arik said. "But not actually."

"Enough." Ochek stood and took out his knife. "Children, walk close to each other, and close to me."

"I think maybe I'll do the same thing," Arik said, and she even took Ochek's paw.

Before long, they came to the base of the mountain range. Their pace had quickened after finding the wolf tracks. There was a good spot to camp where a rock face offered more protection from the wind, and they constructed the hut in record time. All four of them huddled inside, and Eli started a fire for supper. The meal consisted of more dried meat and broth, but it was good to put anything in their stomachs. Ochek took the occasion to make tea for the group: a mix of pine needles, melted snow, and tree sap. As tea went, it was rather bland, like old peppermint gum, but Morgan wasn't about to complain about the warmth it offered. And it had more taste than dried meat, that was certain.

"Is that why you haven't gone this way before?" Eli asked. "Because of the wolf, I mean."

Ochek took a sip of his tea. "When I came this way, a long time ago, trying to find more food for the village, I came across the bridge . . . and the beast. I was too weak to try to fight it, so I left and never came back."

"Because if something happened to you, Misewa wouldn't survive," Eli said.

"Ehe," Ochek said. "It was either be eaten or, if by some miracle I defeated the wolf, get over the mountains and probably find nothing but white. Then I'd have no strength to get back. The outcome would be death no matter what."

"Is the wolf a two-legged animal?" Morgan asked.

"It was walking on four legs," Eli said, "judging by the tracks."

"It was walking on four legs when I saw it before too," Ochek said.

"We can do that, though, if we like," Arik pointed out.

"Yes, we can." Ochek took a bite of dried meat. "I know it's not from Misewa, and that's all. If it *can* walk on two legs . . ."

"Then it can talk? Is that right? Is two legs better than four, or maybe it's the other way around?" Morgan asked.

"I don't know." Ochek put the last bite into his mouth and chewed it thoughtfully. "If it can talk, it can think to set some kind of trap for us. If it can't, it will go on instinct, and I'm not sure that's better."

"Should we just sit here and wait for it to kill us, then?" Morgan immediately wished that she hadn't asked the question. What if they agreed? Then what? Leave in the middle of the night? The dark made her feel empty. Lost. Afraid.

"One wolf won't take on a group of four. When it was only me? That was different," Ochek said. "We'll be safe tonight, and we need the rest."

Morgan felt relieved.

With no wind pummeling their hut, the occasional sound was more pronounced. The crackling of the fire. One of the four chewing meat or slurping broth or tea. Yawns. One time, Eli shifted his body and his back brushed against the hut. Morgan jumped because it sounded like something was outside. Eli admitted it had been him and received a light punch on the arm.

When the fire died down and the meal was done, it was quiet. But even though she was bone-tired, Morgan couldn't sleep. She couldn't stop picturing a wolf charging into the tent, its teeth bared.

She needed a distraction. She forced her thoughts away from the predator and searched for any topic at all that would keep her mind occupied, at least for the night. The question she'd had earlier then occurred to her.

"Do you ever go north?"

"To the woods, you mean?" Ochek asked, propping his head up, eager to talk. Perhaps he couldn't sleep either.

In fact, they all rolled onto their sides, eyes wide open.

"Yeah," Morgan said. "I mean, that's all I could see north of Misewa anyway."

"No," Ochek said. "We don't go into those woods."

"There could be lots of animals to catch there, though, right?" she asked.

"I doubt it," Arik said.

"Why?" Morgan asked. "Because of the Barren Grounds?"

"It's not the Barren Grounds," Ochek explained. "It's what's beyond the Great Tree."

Morgan leaned forward, waiting for Ochek to elaborate. He didn't.

"What's beyond the Great Tree besides woods?" she asked. "More wolves?"

Ochek exchanged a glance with Arik. Morgan tried to read into it, but couldn't.

"*Hello?*" Morgan said. "You're fantasy creatures, not mystery characters."

"Stop it," Eli said. "They obviously don't want to tell us."

"Oh, come on," Morgan said. "We're risking our lives for them and they can't tell us what's in a stupid forest?"

"You don't need to know everything all the time," he said.

"Yes, I do," she said. "And if we get through this and keep living together, you'd better just accept that about me."

"Oh, I like her," Arik said to Ochek.

"*Thank* you," Morgan said.

"Look." Ochek paused and breathed hard through his nose. "There is a giant in those woods, the oldest two-legged one on Askí."

"Mistapew," Arik whispered, as if saying its name out loud might summon it.

Morgan had been scared of the wolf. By the looks on the animal beings' faces, to them, Mistapew made the wolf seem like a bunny rabbit.

"Aren't you going to tell me what *that* means in Cree?" Morgan asked Eli.

"Ochek just said it: giant," Eli said.

"Oh," Morgan said. "Of course. Stupid me."

"There are stories of a time when a group of villagers crossed the Barren Grounds to hunt," Ochek began. "They set up camp outside the forest, at the base of the Great Tree, ready to enter the northern woods the next day. In the dead of night, Mistapew came into their hut. Though it's a giant, it moves like a ghost, and even the best hunters didn't hear it. It took the soul of an Elder, Kihiw, and warned the others never to return. We never have."

"What happened to Kihiw?" Eli asked.

A tear fell from Ochek's eye. "He never woke up."

"Wait a second," Morgan said. "What do you mean, it took Kihiw's soul? How? Where did it put his soul?"

"Nobody knows," Ochek said, "but that's what Mistapew does. It takes your soul and leaves only flesh and bones behind. What makes you who you are is gone, and you are left in a dreamless sleep until you pass away."

"Like a coma," Morgan said.

"What if you found his soul?" Eli asked.

"Then it would be released," Ochek said, "and he would travel into the Happy Hunting Grounds."

"That doesn't sound so happy," Morgan grumbled.

"Have you even . . . looked for the soul?" Eli asked.

Ochek shook his head solemnly. The fire reflected in his eyes. "We've never gone back to the northern woods, only to the tree line. That's how I was able to find you at the Great Tree."

Not another word was said that night. Even Arik had nothing smart to say after Ochek's story, and Morgan wanted to know nothing more about the northern woods, or Mistapew. Eli added the last of the wood to the fire, so that it would burn out during the night, leaving embers to keep them warm until morning.

Morgan was distracted from the wolf, just as she'd wanted to be. But her plan had backfired. She did not sleep any better. She just stared into the fire, and at some point, as the flames died, her consciousness mercifully slipped away with them.

SEVENTEEN

Morgan had a dream. She was standing in the corner of the room again, and the room was lit by a color like the sunset; warm hues spread across the walls like paint. The light came from a lamp resting on a side table. The woman, Morgan's mother, was holding her as a young child. Humming that same song. Humming the song and crying softly, trying not to wake her.

"Kiskisitotaso," the mother whispered to the child. "Kiskisitotaso."

Don't forget about who you are.

Then Morgan *was* the child. She looked up at her mother, reached for her, touched her cheek. Soft. Warm. Damp from crying. Morgan felt tears against her fingertips. The word was spoken over and over, from her mother's lips to her ears.

"Kiskisitotaso."

There was a knock on the front door. Footsteps moved towards it.

"Mwach. Mwach."

Her mother looked towards the bedroom door. She was whispering desperately. It was too late. Morgan heard the front door open. People came inside. She heard angry voices. Her mother stood up from the chair, panicked, repeating, "Mwach! Mwach!" She backed away so quickly that she knocked over the lamp. It fell to the ground and shattered. The light went out, and it was totally black. Morgan wailed in her mother's arms, both of them stuck in the dark.

"Kiskisitotaso," her mother said to her, kissing her cheeks, her nose, her mouth. "Kiskisitotaso."

The door opened, and light flooded into the room. Morgan was standing in the corner of the room again, a teenaged girl. She was crying too, and she watched as a man and a woman came inside. The man held her mother back. The woman took the child from her mother's arms.

"Mwach! Don't take my girl!"

Morgan sat up in a cold sweat. She was back in the hut. The fire had long since gone out, leaving behind charcoaled wood and a chill in the air. It was morning. Daylight seeped into the hut through its stitching. She could see Ochek, Arik, and Eli. They'd been sleeping and stirred now only because of Morgan's outburst.

"What's going on?" Eli asked.

Morgan kept looking around the hut, as though she might be able to see the woman taking the child and stop her. Was the man still holding her mother back? Then she shook her head and closed her eyes tight, willing the vision to leave. She needed to forget the dream, because dreams were meant to be forgotten.

"Nothing," she said. "Sorry."

"You called out 'no' in the good words," Ochek pointed out.

"No, I didn't." Morgan touched her lips in disbelief.

"Yes, you did," Eli said. "Mwach. No."

"I think I'd remember because it came out of my mouth!" Morgan said.

"You might've thought you said 'no' in your language, but it came out in the good words." Arik was stretching joyfully like a cat.

"I need some air." Morgan got up. Her entire body was shaking.

"It's nothing to be ashamed of, Iskwésis," Ochek said.

"It's not that I spoke Cree; it's what I dreamed." Morgan walked to the flap, ready to leave the hut, but stopped there and, despite her best intentions to forget the dream, the *nightmare*, she played it back, clear and full.

"Mwach," she whispered.

Had she said it? The moment she woke up was the only moment she couldn't remember. She pushed the flap open, walked outside, and what she saw there made her scream: wolf tracks circled the outside of the hut, then led away, up the mountain.

The direction they needed to go.

"What is it now?" Ochek asked.

"Tracks." Morgan couldn't take her eyes off the marks in the snow. It was a relatively calm morning, with the sun reflecting off the snow and causing Morgan's eyes to tear up. She wanted wind to push snow over the tracks so she could pretend they were never there. The others came outside and saw the paw prints.

"What do we do?" Morgan asked. "Go back?"

"We can't turn back." Ochek started to take down the hut. "The earlier we start moving, the farther we'll get before dark."

The others helped. When they were finished and had their packs on, Morgan grabbed Eli's hand and held it tightly. She was determined not to let it go as long as they were outside the hut and walking. Arik had the same idea, finding Ochek's paw and clutching it.

Up they went, staying close to one another at all times, which meant that whenever Morgan or Eli fell back, the others did too. There was no wind, which really was a blessing, but the resulting quiet made for an undeniable tension. They heard every sound and were sure that each sound was the wolf stalking them. And it may well have been. More than once, a member of the group thought they saw it pacing behind thick patches of snow-covered pines, which were littered here and there up the mountain. A large beast with dark-gray fur and sun-yellow eyes. But on second look, the wolf was always gone, and they began to wonder whether they were seeing things.

"I don't think we'd all hallucinate the same thing. Like, the *exact* same thing," Morgan pointed out.

Nobody could argue against that.

The higher they went, the harder it was to talk, because while the air had always been cold, it was getting thinner. The mountain sloped gradually but persistently, and they were following the suggestion of a path, which, in the Green Time, might've been an actual path. It wound this way and that, around and through the trees, but always higher, always closer to the summit, which didn't seem any closer than when they'd started out.

"My legs are burning," Morgan said, still walking hand in hand with Eli. "There's this stair-climber in the weight room at school, and this is like going on it and never coming off."

"Mine are too," Eli said.

"It feels like a trap," she said.

"What do you mean, a trap? Like Arik is setting us up?" he asked.

"I can hear you," Arik said in a singsong voice.

"No," Morgan said. "A trap by the wolf."

"It couldn't know we were coming here. Not to begin with," Eli said.

They both took little gasps of air every few words, because of the physical exertion and the ever-thinning air.

"That doesn't mean it's not planning something," she said. "It's circumstance. It's the wolf's good fortune. That's probably how it sees it anyway. Like Ochek when he saw Arik."

"I can *still* hear you," Arik said.

"We can't turn back now," Eli said, echoing what Ochek had said.

"I'm not saying we should. I'm just worried, that's all," Morgan said.

"I am too," he admitted.

They walked for a few more minutes, and then Morgan continued as though they'd never stopped talking. "It's just," she said, "we're climbing up a mountain and we're getting more tired and we're all hungry and who's to say it's not just waiting until we're *too* tired and *too* hungry before it decides it's dinnertime?"

"You don't need to make us *more* worried," Eli said.

They followed the path through a small grove of pine trees. Morgan was thankful each time the path brought them through trees because she could use them to hoist herself forward and upward.

"What if the wolf just pounces on us, even if we're all together? Do you think Ochek could fight it off?"

"I used to go out on the land with my moshom, my grandpa," Eli said. "Sometimes I'd watch the animals with him, just to see what they did. You know, how they went about their day and stuff like that. Watch them build shelters or sleep or eat or hunt, all of that."

"And what's your point?" she asked.

"I saw a fisher once," he said. "It killed a beaver, just like that. The beaver didn't even have a chance."

"A beaver is not a wolf," she said plainly. "Beavers are herbivores, aren't they? Is that supposed to make me feel better?"

"It made me curious about them," he said, "so I started watching videos and reading about them. They're pretty awesome."

"They're talking about you!" Arik tugged on Ochek's paw excitedly.

"Yes." Ochek sighed. "I know they are."

There was truth to what Eli had said. Ochek *was* awesome. After all, an entire village relied on him to provide them with food.

"They even hunt porcupines, you know," he said.

"Really? Even if they get stuck with their quills or what-ever?" she asked.

"I guess," he said.

"I mean," she said, "sure, I guess that's better than a beaver. But still, a porcupine isn't—"

"A wolf. I know," he snapped, obviously frustrated. "How about we just stick together and hope for the best?"

"Stick together." Arik chuckled. "I get it, because of the porcupine and how it can stick somebody with its quills."

"We call that a pun on earth," Morgan said.

"I kind of like that sort of joke," Arik said. "They're very *pun*ny."

"Could you children not encourage her?" Ochek said.

They came through the trees and were back out in the open, headed into a long stretch of undisturbed snow. This was a relief, because it meant that the wolf wasn't near them for the time being, but none of them was foolish enough to think that it had given up its pursuit. The sunlight glittered off the mountainside and it looked like a waterfall of stars.

At the next group of trees, they sat down in the middle of the grove and Eli made a fire. Nearby lay a felled pine tree that was thin and long dead.

"Come, watch here, Iskwésis," Ochek said.

He used a small hatchet to cut the tree into smaller pieces, then had Morgan retrieve two forked sticks from the ground. Together, they cut down a green branch from one of the live trees; Morgan held it down and Ochek chopped it off. Ochek drove the two forked sticks into the ground on either side of the fire and suspended the green stick over the fire with either end of it secured against the forked sticks.

"Wow," she said, "that seemed way harder when I watched you and Eli do that."

"Now you have a spit, so you can cook over the fire," Ochek said. "Well done."

"Thank you," Morgan said proudly. "Next thing you know I'll be making the fires too, and what'll Eli do?"

"Lie back and relax!" Eli laughed, then did just that for a moment.

"There's always something to do," Ochek said.

It was an uneventful lunch. The group noticed their exhaustion only when they finally rested. They sat chewing and sipping in silence until Ochek spoke sharply.

"Get behind me."

He stood tall, making himself look bigger than he had ever looked before. Morgan and Eli and Arik all moved behind him quickly.

There came a growl, low and terrible.

Ochek raised his arms out from his sides protectively, corralling the three others behind him.

Another growl, followed by a sharp bark.

Morgan shuffled to the side and stretched her neck so that she could see over Ochek's shoulder. Eli grabbed her hand, and she thought her hand had never been held tighter. He was either scared or wanting her not to move. Likely both. But then he edged out to the side as well and looked out from behind Morgan.

The wolf was standing on all fours at the end of the grove, between the travelers and the top of the mountain.

Its entire body was covered in dark gray fur, which seemed only there to frame its yellow eyes, more blinding than the sun reflecting off the snowy terrain. Even more pronounced than the wolf's fur or eyes was its size. Beings across Askí were in varying stages of starvation, their fur matted and thin, failing to hide the fact that they had no meat on their bones. The wolf appeared well-fed, a hulk of an animal. Healthy. Its body thick and strong and horrifying.

"It's not from here," Morgan whispered.

"Quiet, Iskwésis," Ochek whispered, his body unmoving.

"She's right," Eli whispered. "Look at it. It's not starving."

"It's from where there's summer," Morgan said.

Each one of them refused to take their eyes off the wolf. The wolf, likewise, didn't take its eyes off the group. It may as well have been a statue, unmoving until ready to strike.

"I heard the summer birds were being held by the man in a cabin just past the mountains," Arik said.

"Those aren't exactly GPS coordinates," Morgan said.

"All we need to do is get past the wolf and over the mountain," Arik said. "Simple."

"*Simple?*" Morgan said. "How are we ever going to make it past that thing?"

"If that's true," Ochek said, "it means the wolf isn't here to eat us now, and it wasn't going to eat me years ago."

"Isn't that what wolves stalk people for?" Morgan asked. "To eat them?"

"It's here to keep us away from the Green Time," Ochek said. "I didn't know it back then, or I might've tried to fight it. I know it now."

At that moment, the wolf rose from its four paws to stand on its hind legs. It straightened out its back with an awful crack, extended its claws, and puffed out its chest. Now standing, with a decidedly evil smirk, it looked bigger than it had before. Its shadow fell over them as if the sky itself had been covered. Ochek reached down, picked up the hatchet he'd used to cut the wood, and clutched it firmly.

"You're right, Ochek." When the wolf spoke, it sounded like he was growling. He had a deep and gravelly voice. "I'm not here to eat you, but I will. Go back to Misewa. You were smart enough to do that before."

"Go back and what? Die?" Ochek asked.

"Die with your village," the wolf said. "It's only right. You've suffered together."

"I'd rather die fighting than die hungry." Ochek pulled out his knife to wield a weapon in either paw.

Anticipating a battle, Arik took one of the hut poles out and wielded it like a Bo staff. Morgan grabbed the end of a piece of wood in the fire and picked it up. A torch was better than nothing. Eli just kept backing away, his heels sliding through the snow, his hands shaking, his eyes wide with fear.

The wolf took one step forward.

"You're with the man," Ochek said. *"Why?"*

"Better there than here, wouldn't you say?" the wolf asked.

"You're a traitor," Ochek said.

"I stay in the Green Time," the wolf said. "And, in turn, I keep the two-legged out."

"That's *exactly* what Ochek meant when he said you were a traitor," Arik said. "You're just agreeing with him."

"This is fun for me. I'm no traitor," the wolf said. "When I'm tired of the man, I'll kill him too."

"Come with us," Ochek said. "Release the summer birds so that we can all live the way we were meant to live."

"And stay with you in your village?" the wolf asked. "Pathetic."

"So . . . that's a no?" Arik said.

"I'll take the Green Time rather than all four seasons in their endless cycle." The wolf took another step forward.

He was now in the grove.

Morgan reached forward with her torch. Arik held her staff out in front of Morgan defensively. Ochek stepped towards the wolf, his weapons at the ready.

The wolf growled and bared his teeth.

"Now," he said, "I gave you a choice."

"There *is* no choice," Ochek said. "If you think you're as vicious as we are determined, shut up and fight."

The wolf looked back and forth across all four of them, sizing each of the travelers up, looking at their weapons, meeting their eyes, and paying particular attention to Eli. This made Morgan step in front of Eli and grab onto her torch with both hands, as if she was holding an ax. The wolf's bright-yellow eyes narrowed as his eyebrows furrowed, and he let out a violent growl, long and sharp. Then he backed out of the grove and dropped to all fours again.

"You'll be at the summit by nightfall," he said. "I'll give you that time as a courtesy, to think about how awful you want your death to be."

"We won't change our minds," Ochek said.

"Then I'll see you very soon," he said.

The wolf strode away from them, slowly and deliberately.

When the wolf was gone, they were finally able to relax, and lowered their weapons.

"You okay?" Morgan asked Eli, who was still shaking.

"Yeah," he said, but his trembling lips and voice said otherwise. "I'm fine."

She dropped the wood back into the fire and took his hand in hers. "We can leave. We can always leave."

"Stop saying that," he said.

"Why didn't he just finish us off?" Ochek asked, more to himself than anybody else, it seemed.

Arik answered anyway. "You heard him. This is sport. He knows he can kill us whenever he wants."

"No," Ochek said. "No, there's something else."

"He can't have been scared of us," Arik said.

"Maybe he feels guilty for what he's doing," Ochek said.

"*That* wolf?" Arik said. "Did we just see the same wolf?"

"Then how would you explain it?"

"Me?" Arik shook her head. "I'm just happy to be alive."

They packed up from lunch without talking about the wolf or the choice he'd given them, left the grove, and continued towards the peak. Now it refused to stay in the distance, forever out of reach, as it had seemed to be earlier in the day. Now it looked closer and closer by the second. Morgan couldn't help but wonder if they were climbing towards their death, rather than Misewa's salvation.

EIGHTEEN

As the sun set on the third day of their journey—and their fifth day on Askí, by Morgan's tally—they reached the summit. Although there was good reason to feel afraid that they'd made it, it was impossible not to appreciate the accomplishment. They came upon a flat area with a perfectly untouched layer of snow where there rested another grove, and at the center of those pine trees stood one tree above all others. A giant sequoia. The tree looked as tall as a mountain itself, the peak of it thrusting into the sky as though you could climb its trunk all the way up to the heavens.

"It's a good place to eat dinner and rest," Ochek said as they walked through the trees.

They found that the pines had given the sequoia space enough to allow their hut to be erected near its base.

"I bet you can see the entire world from up here," Morgan said, and to test her theory, she kept walking until she came to the other side of the grove, then farther, to the edge of the summit.

She looked out over the land they were headed to, and was soon joined by Eli. They saw, only a few miles away, an end to the White Time. It looked like a lake of greens and browns coming up against a beach of white sand. Morgan reached her hands towards it, as if she could gather in the warmth right there. So did Eli.

"You were right, Arik!" he called out.

Not long after, Arik and Ochek emerged from the grove. Once Ochek saw the Green Time, he buried his face in his paws and began to cry.

Even Arik was quiet at first, looking over the land. "I knew they were right," she whispered.

"Knew who were right?" Morgan asked. "Who would've told you about this and not have done something about it themselves?"

"Oh, that's neither here nor there," Arik said quickly.

"It is if it means we never had to—"

"None of your concern," she interrupted. "They had their reasons. The point is, we've found it."

Ochek stared at the land below. It was such a beautiful thing to see him like that that both Morgan and Eli started to watch only him. They looked away only when Ochek appeared to gather himself.

He said in the most level voice he could manage, "Let's eat, then sleep. Tomorrow, we'll find the man."

"I can see his place right from here." Arik pointed directly west, where, against the horizon, the sun was falling out of view.

There was a line across the land where the white turned to greens and browns, where the frozen lake broke off and its sky-blue waters rushed into a forest so rich that you couldn't see the ground if you tried. Beyond the forest, there was a smaller river that fed into an enormous lake in the shape of a perfect circle. In the middle of the lake, on a small island, was a house. Even from where they were, at the top of the mountain, they could see light shining out from within the cabin like miniature sunbeams.

"There are your summer birds," Arik said.

Ochek assessed the space between here and there and said confidently, "By this time tomorrow, we'll have set them free."

"Not so tasty now, am I?" she asked.

"You were right, dear Arik," he said. "You were right."

The four stood at the edge of the mountaintop until they had to pry themselves away from the view to finish setting up camp. A feeling of excitement came over them, as they thought this might be the last time they'd set up camp in the freezing cold. There was real hope now, as sure as the sun would rise in the morning, and not one of them mentioned why they'd been so scared earlier in the day.

Not one of them spoke of the wolf at all.

They ate supper quietly and quickly and packed up everything they could before turning in for the night so they could leave promptly in the morning. It was only when they were lying down, encircling the fire, that they talked—precisely when they planned to be sleeping. They were all too excited.

"My father was still alive back then," Ochek said. "Before the man left with the summer birds."

"How many people were in Misewa?" Morgan asked.

"There were children, parents, Elders . . ."

"I'm sorry," Eli said.

"My father was going to take me out on the land." Ochek poked at the fire with no real purpose. "We went to bed early so that we could get up and leave before the others woke. My father told me that if I caught anything, we'd have a feast. I was excited. I *knew* I was going to catch something." Ochek let go of his stick and watched as it erupted into a small flame and then collapsed into the fire. "It was a perfect day, right in the middle of the Green Time. The White Time had passed and wouldn't be back until two seasons had gone by."

Ochek lay on his back and looked up through the small opening at the top of the hut. You could see one star through the opening, and the smoke escaping through it. Morgan and Eli and Arik stayed still and silent, waiting for him to continue.

"When I woke up that morning, it didn't feel right. It was dark, when the sun should've been rising. Nobody had set a fire because the weather had been warm, and it was cold in the lodge. And the wind. The wind was violent outside, whistling in through the cracks in the wood. I . . ." Ochek's voice began to break, and he started again only when he'd righted it. "I opened the door, went outside, and it was the White Time. The green, the earth, the waters—washed away in a flood of snow and ice. Soon after, we learned that the man had gone with the summer birds and Tahtakiw."

"And the rest is history," Arik said.

"No." Ochek sat up looking determined, his eyes burning with intensity. "It *will* be history after tomorrow. The Elders will paint it on the walls, and we'll tell stories about it to our children, and our children's children."

"Say what you will about Captain Serious over here," Arik said, "but he can sure give a speech, right?"

"And you can sure kill a mood." Morgan chuckled.

"I remember hunting with my moshom," Eli said, and everybody was just as quiet for him as they had been for Ochek. "I was too young to carry a rifle, so he gave me a slingshot. We were hunting for moose, but he told me to use the slingshot if I saw something small enough. Moshom had a moose caller made out of birch, and he sounded just like one, but the moose weren't coming. We looked for them the whole day, and when it was night, we started back home. That's when I saw a prairie chicken just crossing the path in front of us. I pulled out my sling-shot . . ." At this point, Eli ghosted the act of using his slingshot. He pulled the sling back, closed one eye to aim, then let go. "And I hit it. It was just a little thing, but my moshom was so proud. We carried it back to the house and he invited all our relatives over and we had a feast. He cut up that bird in the tiniest pieces so everybody could have some."

Morgan reached over and wiped Eli's tear away. She kept her thumb against his cheek. "You're a good kid."

"I miss him," he said.

"I know." What she said next surprised her, as though she hadn't even said it. "I miss her too."

As soon as Morgan had said those four words—at once the most simple and profound words she'd spoken in her life—she wondered if she really did miss her mother. She hated her, didn't she? Her mother had let her go, hadn't she? But Morgan had dreamed something different. This was what Morgan thought about as she lay on her side, facing the fire. She thought of her mother, of Eli's moshom, of family, while her eyelids became heavy. This was Morgan's last thought before she fell asleep.

Kiskisitotaso. Kiskisitotaso. Kiskisitotaso.

"Kiskisitotaso," her mother whispered, as clearly as though she was lying beside Morgan, her lips against her daughter's ear. "Kiskisitotaso."

There was a knock on the door. There were footsteps. Her mother was backing away from the bedroom door, knocking over the lamp. It was black. The deepest night.

"Noooooo!" somebody screamed.

It wasn't her mother.

When her mother had screamed that night, she'd said it in Cree. *Mwach. No.* The word hadn't come from Morgan's mouth either, as she watched the scene unfold before her.

"Noooooo!" The scream came again.

It wasn't from the nightmare at all. It wasn't Morgan remembering. It was Eli. Clear. Terrified. Had he been dreaming as well? Had he been having a nightmare? Morgan catapulted into a sitting position in time to see Eli being dragged out of the hut by the wolf, his eyes burning bright yellow.

He had his jaws around Eli's ankle.

"Morgan, help!" he cried.

Eli dug his fingers into the hide that the hut was made of, but was unable to stop himself from being dragged away. Morgan lunged towards him. Her fingertips brushed against his, but she was too late. In a moment, Eli was gone. Dragged into the black. You would never have known he was there if his screams hadn't pierced through the silence of the night. If the wolf's eyes weren't still visible in the otherwise endless darkness.

Morgan knelt at the entrance to the hut, too shocked to move.

"Morgan!" Eli's screams were farther away by the second.

Morgan looked back and saw that Ochek and Arik were waking up now, startled and confused. She wanted to wait for them to get up and save Eli. For them to go out into the dark, not her. She could hear the woman taking her, as a toddler, out of the pitch-black room. Her footsteps. Her own screams. Her mother's screams. *Mwach.* The man telling her mother to calm down or else he'd handcuff her to the doorknob. *Mwach.* She wasn't in a dream. She was here, now, and Eli was getting taken.

Eli was screaming.

She had been scared of the black for too long.

Morgan reached for a piece of half-burning wood, ran out of the hut, and into the night. She kept running in the direction of Eli's desperate cries for help, and the wolf's growling. Was it already too late? Was he already being eaten? Her torch offered no more than a glow, like a dying flashlight. Trees came at her suddenly from the black. She dodged them and kept running, trying not to slow down.

Then she was out of the grove.

"Morgan!"

Eli's voice was hoarse from screaming. He sounded tired and weak.

"I'm coming!" Morgan called back.

She rushed towards the sound of his voice until she could see the wolf standing over Eli, his front paws pinning the boy's shoulders down, his hind paws pressing down against Eli's shins. Morgan saw the wolf's drool land on Eli's cheek. Eli's head was turned away from the beast, and he was looking directly at Morgan with terror. She could see his chest heaving up and down, his skin pale and sweaty.

Morgan didn't hesitate. She sprinted towards Eli and the wolf until she was right up to them, and swung at the wolf with her torch. The fire connected with the wolf's side. He yelped and fell off Eli. Eli quickly scampered behind her, clutching her hips.

"You okay?" she asked while keeping her eyes on the wolf.

Eli's grip tightened around Morgan in response.

The wolf rose to his hind legs, standing like a human. "Remember. You asked for this to happen."

"Leave us alone!" Morgan demanded.

"Let me have the boy and I'll let you all turn around and go back to Misewa," he said.

"Mwach!" Morgan screamed.

She threw the torch at the wolf. The wood hit the animal's face. He yelped again and held his front paws over the wound.

"Run!" Morgan shouted to Eli.

They both ran away from the wolf, through the trees, and back towards the hut. They could hear the wolf give chase. When they ran into the clearing where their hut and the sequoia were, Ochek and Arik were there. Ochek had a torch in one paw and the hatchet in the other. Arik had both paws wrapped firmly around her makeshift Bo staff.

"Get in the hut!" Ochek said to the kids.

Morgan and Eli ran past the animal beings but stopped outside of the hut and turned around in time to see the wolf leap into the clearing from behind the trees. He looked like a black cloud, a storm bearing down on them. A storm with two lightning bolts for eyes. Ochek took a mighty swing at the wolf as he came down on them, and Arik screamed as the wolf landed on top of Ochek. They slammed against the ground and started rolling around, fighting and gnashing and growling. The wolf opened his considerable jaws, baring his teeth, and lunged towards Ochek's throat, but Arik stuck the end of her Bo staff into the wolf's mouth.

The wolf reached out and grabbed the staff from Arik. It was the distraction Ochek needed. He took another swing with his hatchet, and the blade landed between the wolf's shoulder and throat. A mist of blood splashed against the white snow. The wolf yelped once more, then fell in a heap. The animal tried to get to his feet, but failed. Tried to go onto all fours, but collapsed onto his belly. He started to pull himself away, out of the clearing and into the woods, leaving a trail of blood behind. Ochek calmly walked after the wolf. When he came to the beast, he raised the hatchet into the air and readied a killing strike.

"No!" Eli ran over to Ochek. He jumped up, grabbed Ochek's arm, and pulled it down.

"What are you doing, boy? He tried to kill you!" Ochek said.

"And now you're about to kill him!"

"So that he doesn't return and kill us all!" Ochek said. "This is not like before!"

"He can't even walk!" Morgan stepped between Ochek

and the wolf and was soon followed by Eli. "It's not like he can do anything to hurt us now."

"Move," Ochek demanded.

"Mwach," Eli said.

Morgan could see that Eli was shaking, but he stayed in place, staunch in his protection of the animal.

"Please, Ochek," the wolf croaked while crawling away from them, slow and pathetic. His breathing was labored, and blood started to pool around his body, staining the perfect white with deep red. He looked at Ochek with pale-yellow eyes, a suggestion of what they used to be.

Ochek pushed through Morgan and Eli, then stood over the wolf, hatchet raised in the air once more.

The wolf drew his paws over his face, a sad and futile gesture.

Ochek paused.

"Please," Eli said.

Morgan looked away from the two animal beings, not willing to watch.

"Forgive me," the wolf whispered.

Ochek tilted his head, then lowered the hatchet. He went down on one knee and rested his elbow against it. The hatchet dropped to the ground with a thud.

"What did you say?"

"Forgive me," the wolf said, like a weak and distant wind.

Morgan walked over to Ochek and the wolf. In Ochek's eyes she saw a look of familiarity, as though this had all happened before. Soon, all three of the travelers were watching Ochek. The hunter's eyes were searching, darting back and forth, before settling on the wolf.

The wounded predator lowered his paws, rested them at his sides.

"Do it, then," the wolf said.

"No."

The wolf turned away to stare into the black of night. He breathed heavily once. Twice. "Why?"

Ochek picked up the hatchet and slid it under his belt. He sighed. "Where's the sport in killing something so wretched?"

"Coward," the wolf said.

"What's taking a boy from a hut in the middle of the night, you jerk?" Morgan said. "You're the coward!"

"I would've let the rest of you go," the wolf said. "I call that mercy."

"You know nothing of mercy." Ochek slipped his paws underneath the wolf's great body and lifted him to his feet.

NINETEEN

O chek tended to the wolf's wounds. Arik watched with great interest and occasionally fetched one thing or another from Ochek's pack. Morgan wasn't interested so much in what Ochek was doing. She wasn't even sure that she wanted the wolf to live. Instead, she kept wondering to herself: if they saved the wolf, what would stop him from stalking them again? Had she and Eli made a mistake in pleading for the beast's life? Having the wolf mere feet away from the both of them didn't help matters. It caused Morgan to question things all the more.

Eli remained terrified.

"You okay?" she asked.

She had her arms wrapped protectively around him. She craned her neck around to see his face. He was staring at the animal. At the gaping wound. At his open mouth and razor-sharp teeth. Maybe picturing his own blood on the ground, rather than the wolf's. What could have been.

"I don't want him to die," he whispered. "I don't want anybody to die."

For a moment, the only sound was the wolf's labored breathing.

"If he dies, he dies," Morgan said. "We did everything we could. He kind of did it to himself."

"Ochek would've just—"

"Ochek was protecting you," Morgan said. "He was protecting all of us."

They watched Ochek work. He looked as though he were conducting a symphony, the way his paws moved fluidly from one task to another. He'd brought medicines with him, and he'd ground those medicines in a bowl with a tool that looked like a miniature baseball bat. From there, he'd made a paste with sap and snow, suspending it over the fire until it began to bubble. With the paste ready, he covered the wolf's wounds with it, the ones inflicted by his hatchet and the torches. Arik administered strips of hide to the wounds. Finally, Ochek made tea for the wolf using different medicines and pine. He hung the pot over the fire using the spit, and there was nothing else to do while they waited for the water to boil.

Morgan and Eli stared at the wolf while the wolf struggled to breathe, groaning every once in a while. Each time he groaned, he placed his paw over the hatchet wound. Blood was soaking through the strip of hide Arik had placed there. Seeing the red stains forming on the hide, Arik approached the wolf and applied pressure on the wound to try to stem the flow of blood. The wolf snarled and swatted at Arik, and she only narrowly dodged the strike.

"You're going to bleed to death, dumb wolf." Arik said, stubbornly staying where she was, her paws pressed down on the wound.

"What do you care?" the wolf asked.

Arik pressed down the slightest bit harder and it made the wolf moan and look away from the wound. When he did, his eyes met Eli's.

"What do any of you care?" the wolf asked.

"I . . ." Eli started with a trembling voice, but he couldn't force out more than that one sound.

"What are you staring at, boy?" the wolf growled through the pain.

"N-nothing," Eli said.

"You don't want anybody to die," the wolf uttered, repeating what Eli had just said. "You want *me* to die, child. I would want the same thing."

"I don't," Eli said. "I wouldn't."

The wolf kept his sickly yellow eyes on him, then looked to the opening at the top of the hut where the poles met. "You might get your wish anyway, even though you won't admit it."

"Stop being such a baby," Morgan said. "I never thought I'd hear a wolf pouting. *Holy.*"

"At least the girl speaks what's on her mind," the wolf said.

"I never wanted you to die!" Eli raised his voice, which seemed to startle the wolf.

"There it is." The wolf tried to laugh but coughed out blood. "Anger."

"Why are you so mean?" Eli asked. "We're trying to help you!"

"I never asked for your help," the wolf said.

"Yeah, you did. You *literally* asked for forgiveness!" Morgan said.

The wolf blinked a tear of pain out of the corner of his eye.

In the silence, Arik changed the dressing on the wolf's wound, adding a fresh strip of hide. She placed her paws on top of the new dressing, and the wolf grimaced, baring his teeth for a moment.

The water started to boil, and Ochek took the small pot down. He stirred the liquid around before pouring it into a cup for the wolf. He helped the wolf raise his head, and with care he tipped the cup towards the beast's mouth. The wolf swallowed, and even that seemed to cause him agony.

"I might be mean," the wolf said to Eli, "but you're weak. What would you rather be?"

"How about just nice," Morgan said, "rather than either?"

"Who's the one who's weak right now?" Eli said.

The wolf looked at Eli contemplatively, and then there was a spark in his yellow eyes. "Maybe I was wrong," the wolf admitted. "When you talk to me like that, I think maybe you can change."

"Leave him alone," Morgan said.

"You'll see," the wolf said. "The world will harden you." He nodded, as though agreeing with himself.

Eli shook his head. "If I can change, then you can change."

The wolf chuckled, and more blood dripped from the corners of his mouth. Arik dabbed at it.

"Ridiculous boy," the wolf whispered.

"Look at you," Eli said, "trying to kill us and nearly getting killed, if it hadn't been for me. Who's ridiculous?"

"Leave me be," the wolf said. "Awas."

In the morning, after they had all woken up and had breakfast, the wolf seemed to have turned a corner. He ate a small portion of food, his breathing was easier, and his eyes were a brighter yellow. But when he tried to get up after eating, he cried out and collapsed onto his back. He would live, but he was still weak and seemed in too much pain to go anywhere or do anything. For the four travelers, this meant it was safe to go.

"We'll leave you the hut," Ochek said.

They'd packed up everything they would need to sustain themselves before entering the Green Time, where the land would provide for them. They were all standing outside by the opening of the hut, while the wolf remained inside on the ground, by the fire.

"Tonight, we'll be in the Green Time," Ochek continued, "and I haven't slept under the stars since I was young."

"How adorable," the wolf said dryly.

"Don't make me regret my choice. If you approach us on our way back . . ."

"I'll do what's in my nature," the wolf warned.

"As long as it's not what your master told you to do."

Ochek didn't wait for the wolf to say anything back. He just turned away and started walking. Arik followed him, and the two animal beings made their way through the grove and into the open, where they would start on their way to the man's cabin.

Eli stayed behind, and, seeing this, Morgan remained with him. But she hung back at what felt like a safe distance.

"Awas," the wolf said.

"I'll go away in a minute," Eli said.

"I could kill you right now, sick and all."

"I don't think you will."

Hearing the threat, Morgan stepped closer to the pair.

"You don't know me," the wolf said.

The wolf and the boy kept their eyes on each other, Eli standing at the entrance to the hut and the wolf lying inside.

"Your bandages need changing," Eli said.

"I'll do it myself," the wolf said.

"Here." Eli crouched down to enter the hut.

"Hey, what are you doing?" Morgan grabbed Eli's shoulder.

"It's okay," he said to her. "Trust me."

"It's not you I don't trust," she said.

"He won't do anything." Eli's eyes were full of determination and assuredness. Unblinking.

Morgan removed her hand from his shoulder.

Eli entered the hut, knelt beside the wolf, and took off the bandage, which was soaked with blood.

"I could rip your throat out right now, you know," the wolf said.

"Do it if you're going to," Eli said, "or be quiet and let me finish dressing your wound."

He placed a new strip of hide atop the wound, and walked out of the hut.

"What's your name, boy?" the wolf asked, which stopped Eli in his tracks.

"Eli. What's yours?"

"Mahihkan."

Eli just nodded at Mahihkan, then he and Morgan ran off through the grove to catch up with their companions. They were standing at the edge of the summit, waiting for them.

TWENTY

It was like another world on the other side of the mountain. There were more trees, as though they'd come to bask in the air and they were fully alive. The snow was damp and shallow, and halfway down the mountain they came across a stream that had formed as it melted. They would find, as they went farther, that the stream fed into the river they'd spotted from atop the mountain. They began shedding layers of clothing and eventually stuffed all the winter clothing into one of their packs and left it hanging on a tree, to be retrieved on their way back to Misewa.

The journey itself was faster, not only because they were heading down a mountain, not up it, and not because the weather was forgiving, but because they were excited for what was happening around them and what lay ahead.

By midmorning they'd come to the foot of the mountain, and they stopped there to eat. They made it a quick meal so they could get back on foot and to the cabin as soon as possible. Nobody seemed to care that this meal was the last meal their rations could provide for them.

"This is how it used to be," Ochek said after they started walking again. Patches of grass were sticking out through the snow. "The closer we are to the Green Time, the more I can remember." He bent down and picked a blade of grass from the ground. "When we were out on the land, we had only the next meal. If we didn't catch anything, we didn't eat. It's the way it was, kayas."

"Long ago," Eli translated for Morgan.

"What he's trying to say, in his Ochek way, is not to worry," Arik said, "if you were worried at all."

"I've been on the land, just like this," Eli said.

"*You* were happy on the land when the land was only snowflakes and ice," Ochek said.

"It all feels like home," Eli said. "If I had a choice, though, it wouldn't be in the middle of a blizzard."

"Oh, good," Morgan said. "At least I know you're not bonkers, even though it looked like you were trying to make friends with that wolf."

"Everybody deserves a second chance," Ochek answered before Eli could.

As they got farther down the mountain, they could see an actual path in front of them that wound through the woods, and the thin line of water they'd seen on the mountain had now formed into a brook. Seeing, for the first time, an opportunity to drink something other than melted snow, they rushed over to the fresh water. Morgan and Eli drank so much that they felt like bursting. It was cold and refreshing and like nothing they'd tasted before.

"We'll find something for dinner," Ochek said. "The water means there'll be four-legged ones."

"I won't have to steal from your traps anymore!" Arik said.

"And *I* won't have to almost eat you."

"I guess we're all happy, then, aren't we?" Arik shoved Ochek playfully. "However, I have a feeling you just might miss me, oh grumpy one."

"Hmmm." Ochek grinned. "You just might be right, oh annoying one."

At midday, they came to the place they'd seen from the mountain, where the snow ended, almost in a straight line, and gave way to the Green Time. They stood there with their toes on the line and pointing towards the thick, long grass, the brook and the flowers by its banks, and the trees with their fullness. It was all too much for Ochek. He placed his paws on the other side of the line before anything else, then his forehead, and he started to sob. The other three knelt beside him and placed their hands on him for comfort.

The land had started to come alive as they'd walked down the side of the mountain, but where they were now, the warmth really began. Morgan stroked Ochek's back, his body now half in the Green Time and half on the other side, and she could feel the difference in temperature on the back of her hand. On one side of the line, it was like a cool day in spring. On the other side, a summer day in June. The other two must have noticed this, because soon they weren't comforting Ochek but testing the sensation of moving their hands from one side of the line to the other. Then all at once they started to laugh, and even Ochek's sobs turned to deep laughter.

The animal being straightened himself but was unwilling to fully cross over the line, as though it was a sacred place. Wonder and awe stuck in the air and fell over them, just the weight of it, until a snowball struck the back of Ochek's head.

He whipped around, more surprised than angry. "What was th—?"

As soon as Ochek had spoken, and before he could react, another snowball connected with his face. Bits of snow clung to his fur. Now he did look angry, but this lasted only until he saw Eli's enormous smile, which was infectious. He'd backed away from the group into the cold side, without any of them noticing.

Ochek licked away the snow. "Just what do you think you're doing?"

"It's a snowball!" Eli said. "Try it!"

"But we have important work left to—"

Another snowball hit Ochek on the shoulder. Morgan had a mischievous look on her face and snow on her hands. Eli and Morgan reloaded with a snowball, swiping their hands across the ground and fashioning the collected snow into perfectly round balls.

"It looks like we have a mutiny!" Arik stood beside Ochek. She'd watched how the foster siblings had made their weapons, and she'd made one of her own. She held it at the ready.

"It appears that we do." Ochek made one too.

And there the four of them were, the animal beings side by side and facing the humans. Each had a snowball in hand, cocked and ready to throw. Each side waited for the other to make the first move.

What followed was the most epic snowball fight that has ever been fought, either on earth or Askí, with both teams standing strong, bravely getting hit, throwing as many as possible at the same time, and laughing the whole way through. And, at least for the time being, there was not a care in the world; the wolf was at the top of the mountain, recovering from his wounds, and the man was still too far away to hear their battle.

When it was over, all four of them ended up on the ground laughing hysterically, with the area between them completely cleared of snow as they'd used it all for snowballs. They were soaking wet and their stomachs hurt from laughing, and each one of them was utterly distracted from the last, and most crucial, part of their journey.

Eventually, without a word exchanged between the four, just knowing looks, they remembered what needed to be done and felt ready for it. It was like their fun had given them the energy of a full night's rest. They got up, stood side by side with their toes on the line, crossed over it, and continued towards the cabin.

They didn't head there directly.

Ochek made a point of stopping several times and didn't seem to care about prolonging the last leg of their journey. He stopped at the banks of the river to pull sweetgrass, because all they had back at Misewa was one braid of it in the Council Hut. He stopped to eat berries at a tree and to load some in his backpack to bring home to the Elders. He stopped to collect some cedar leaves and bark, which he stored with the sweetgrass.

"I've not seen any of these things fresh since before the White Time," he explained.

They weren't more than a hundred yards from the lake that surrounded the island the man's house was on when Ochek stopped again. This time, it wasn't to marvel at the most mundane thing, like a dandelion or something of the sort. Rather, he had a confused look on his face, which soon gave way to concern as he carefully observed the world around them, as far as he could see.

"What is it?" Eli asked.

"There's no game," Ochek said. "Not a four-legged creature on the land, not a bird in the sky, not one fish in the water. Nothing." He turned towards them. "Have any of you seen anything?"

None of them had.

"Maybe we just missed them all," Morgan said.

"You only just now started really looking, after all," Arik pointed out.

"Well, look now," Ochek demanded.

They scanned the area carefully. The water and the sky and the land. They could see a long way in every direction. Ochek was right. There was no game to be seen and so no game to be caught.

"This doesn't make sense," Morgan said. "Where could they have gone? Where else would they go?"

She ran over to the river and peered into the water, hoping to see something, anything. But the river was empty, just like the land, just like the sky. She sat on the riverbank.

The others sat beside her.

Arik put her paw on Ochek's shoulder. "No pisiskiw in their right mind would leave a place like this. Heck, I'm not sure I'm going to come back with you three." She chuckled, but when nobody laughed, she must have realized it wasn't the time for jokes. She turned serious. "There has to be another reason why they've all gone, is what I'm trying to say. It doesn't mean that when we bring the Green Time back to Misewa, there won't be yummy things to eat."

"I'm not sad because I think they've left," Ochek said. "I don't think they've run away anywhere."

"So, do you think they're all playing an elaborate game of hide-and-seek?" Arik asked.

"That's stupid," Morgan said.

"They're dead," Eli said.

Ochek took a long breath in and let it out. "The boy's right. They're not hiding, and they haven't run away. They've been killed."

"What?" Morgan said. "By the man?"

"*Humans.*" Ochek watched the swift water pass them by for a moment that seemed to stretch on. "The land provides everything that anybody would need. If you take only what you need, the land renews itself so that it can provide more. Medicines, water, plants, meat. In exchange, because we don't really have anything the land wants, we honor it for what it gives us." Ochek turned towards Arik and the children. "When you take more than the land can provide, it stops giving. It *can't* give. That's what's happened here. That's what happens with humans."

"You mean us?" Eli asked.

Ochek nodded regretfully.

"That's crap!" Morgan said. "We've been here with you for so long now, and all we've done is help!" She stood up to face Ochek eye to eye. "We haven't taken anything more than what was given! Not every human is the same!"

"Maybe you just haven't had a chance to show me otherwise," Ochek said.

"What have we shown you already?" Eli asked.

"The man came here and was accepted," Ochek said. "He showed us what you have shown me. And then he showed us his true nature."

"We wouldn't take more than we need!" Morgan shouted. She heard her mother whisper to her in that moment. *Kiskisitotaso.* For the first time, she felt she knew something about herself that she'd long forgotten: she belonged in a place like this. She belonged on the land. She'd never felt more at home than during the days she'd spent on Aski.

"Don't make us go," Eli pleaded. "That's what you're saying, right?"

Ochek looked at them intensely, first Morgan, then Eli. "Maybe you aren't the same as the man. The others that came before the man, they were Indigenous, like you both. They never wavered."

"We won't either," Morgan said.

"Iskwésis," Ochek said, "since embarking on this journey, you've said, more than once, that you and Eli could go home, that you *should* go home."

"I know, but . . ."

"I'll give you the choice right now. Go home, where it's safe, and where this place will live on in the stories that you tell one another. You will always be welcome in Misewa."

"This isn't like Hawaii, some place you go just because the weather's bad in Winnipeg," Eli said. "Misewa feels more like home than either of those places."

"What are these places? Hawaii and Winnipeg? I thought you both came from earth?" Arik said.

"It's like Askí is earth, and Misewa is Winnipeg," Morgan said. "Something like that."

"And this Hawaii?" Arik asked.

"Like the South Country?" Morgan tried. "Is there a South Country? There's got to be, right?"

"Iskwésis . . ." Ochek said.

"Right," Morgan said. "You're right." She *had* said that they could go home, more than once. They could have turned around at any point and gone back to earth. *Maybe we* should *go*, she thought. How much harder could it be to defeat a human, after they'd defeated a wolf? Ochek and Arik could do it without them, couldn't they? Shouldn't they? What if something happened to Eli? What would she ever say to James and Katie? Eli was her responsibility. And Ochek had said it himself: they would always be welcome here. They could come, minus the danger.

"Morgan," Eli said, "why are you even thinking about this?"

"Because I'm your big sister and I have to think about keeping you safe. That's my job," she said.

"You're my big sister?" he asked.

"That just sort of came out," she said, "but yeah." She looked him over. Thought about all the time they'd spent together, everything they'd gone through. She didn't want to be without him. Here, or on earth. "Yeah, you're my brother."

"Then don't make me leave here," Eli said. "Please."

"They can do it without us," Morgan reasoned, echoing the thoughts she'd just run through in her mind.

"No," Arik said. "We can't."

"How would you even know that?" Morgan asked.

"You'll see," Arik told her. "One day."

Ochek extended his paw. "Come with us, then. We have a lot left to do."

Eli's face was all Morgan needed to see. If he really was her little brother, then how could she ever live with herself if she made them leave now? Maybe Arik was right. Maybe they, Arik and Ochek, really couldn't do it without them. Could they have overcome the wolf on their own? And what if Ochek had killed Arik? She and Eli had stopped him. The White Time would never have had a chance to end. If there was a chance it still might not, was there a choice at all?

Morgan took Ochek's paw.

TWENTY-ONE

With the sun beginning its descent, the lake was like a sheet of glass and mirrored the sky overhead. Blue had been replaced with the fiery hues of autumn. Deep reds and oranges and yellows rolled over the water in waves. Across the water, at the center of the lake, was the island, and on it, the house. There was a canoe docked on the island shore, paddles resting on the ground beside it, and a brilliant light was emitted from within the dwelling. A rack for smoking meat outside the entrance to the house, not unlike the ones in Misewa but poorly constructed, was empty. The man, it seemed, wasn't immune to the lack of game.

"It's good that we've come now," Ochek said. The group was at the shore, looking out over the water and towards the house. "Soon, the man will move on if there is nothing left to eat here. He will move on, and on, until there's nowhere left to move on to."

"I'd say, if that's the case, this is something we're doing not just for Misewa, but for all of Askí," Arik said.

"No pressure," Ochek said.

Morgan and Eli exchanged a surprised look. Morgan wasn't sure if she'd actually heard what she thought she had.

"Ochek, did you just make a joke?" she asked.

"You children must be rubbing off on me." Ochek took a step into the lake. "Now, remember, swim with your heads just above the water. It's getting dark enough that if he looks out, he may not see us."

"And if he sees us?" Eli asked.

"We're sitting sisipak," Arik said.

"*That* means 'ducks,'" Morgan beat Eli to the translation this time. "Sitting ducks."

They waded into the lake, leaving their packs on the shore, and the children in particular were pleased that the water was warm. Morgan recalled the first week she'd been placed with Katie and James. Before school started, they'd taken her out to Grand Beach, about an hour outside of Winnipeg. The beach stretched endlessly along the water, and the sand was white and soft and hot. But the water wasn't. Near the end of summer, the lake still felt terribly cold, and it took several minutes before her body adjusted to the temperature. She wasn't sure it ever did. But this was like swimming in lukewarm bathtub water, the kind of warmth you get after you've been sitting in the tub for an hour. It made the swim as pleasant as it could be, given the circumstances.

They swam with their noses above the water, and sometimes with their noses below the water, after big gulps of air. If the man looked out from the window, he might see something that looked more like driftwood than animals and human beings. This was especially important now, seeing as how his meat rack was empty and the game was scarce or absent entirely in this area of the North Country. Morgan worried that he might make like Ochek and try to eat one of his own.

It wasn't far from the land to the island, but the journey was long nonetheless, because they were all dog-paddling, trying their best not to disturb the water or rise too far above the surface. Eventually they came to the island and emerged from the water under cover behind the canoe. There had been no movement from within the cabin, just the light and heat showering out of it. They remained behind the canoe, their backs against the hull, out of sight from the cabin, just in case the man happened to look out the window.

"Arik," Ochek whispered. "Go and peek inside the cabin, very quietly."

"Duh," Arik whispered back. She crawled across the grass on all fours towards the house.

They watched as she positioned herself underneath the window, then slowly rose up until she was just high enough to see inside. Suddenly she collapsed onto all fours and scurried back over to the canoe.

"The birds are in a sack hanging from the ceiling," Arik reported. "Tahtakiw, the traitor crane, is perched at the foot of the man's bed, right under the sack. Warm and happy as a clam."

"Wait. Perched?" Morgan tried to think if Oho had been perched. They were kind of sitting in the Council Hut, more than perched. But still, very owllike. "Isn't Tahtakiw a being like you two are? Why isn't he, you know, sitting in a chair or something? How does it work with birds?"

"Pinésisak that can talk are mostly just like pinésisak that can't," Arik explained.

"Or else they couldn't fly, I'd think," Ochek added.

"Yes, they'd be much too big," Arik said. "I think the only difference would be that they have these . . . " Arik made her paw into a weird, clawlike shape. "Feathery fingers. Honestly, they're kind of weird. But they can grab things anyway."

"Oho always has the cane with them," Ochek said.

"Right?" Arik said. "It's funny that they can probably fly perfectly fine, but need a cane to walk."

"They don't fly much, but you're right. I suspect when the White Time is over, they'll fly out of joy," Ochek said.

"Alright so Tahtakiw's perched. I get it," Morgan said. "You guys kind of overexplained that."

"Hey, you're the one who needs to know everything, Iskwésis," Arik said. "According to your dear brother."

"I mean, she has a point," Eli said. "You do need to know everything."

"Gang up on the curious girl, why don't you," Morgan said.

"And the man?" Ochek asked, trying to steer the conversation back on track. "What is he doing?"

Arik cleared her throat. "Sleeping."

"Good." Ochek scanned the group, one by one, with fierce determination. "A sack, you say?"

"Yes, like the empty one you had when you tried to kill me," Arik explained.

"Thanks for reminding me." Ochek rolled his eyes. "The summer birds being in a sack makes things easier actually."

"What do we do?" Morgan watched as Ochek's black eyes darted back and forth.

"Okay," he whispered, "I have a plan."

The other three leaned in, and Ochek went over each of their roles in retrieving the summer birds from the cabin. They broke off and took their positions.

Eli, with great caution, pushed the canoe into the water, placed the paddles inside the vessel, and held it in place, ready for their escape.

Arik crept along the shoreline until she was right out in the open, and she waited there.

Ochek and Morgan ducked low, crossed over the grass and stopped underneath the window. Ochek handed Morgan a thin strip of fabric he'd torn from his clothing and made into a slipknot.

"Ready, Iskwésis?"

She gripped the fabric in her fist. "Ready."

Ochek nodded at Eli, then at Arik. Seeing the signal, Eli got into the canoe and angled it to face northeast, away from the dying sun, towards Misewa. Once Eli was set and keeping the canoe aimed properly with one of its paddles, Arik got to her feet, cupped her mouth, and started making "*Pssst!*" sounds towards the house, doing her best to get Tahtakiw's attention while trying not to wake the man.

It worked.

There was rustling inside the dwelling; it was Tahtakiw flapping his wings, moving from his spot at the foot of the bed to the window. "What's going on out here?" As soon as he appeared in the window, poking his head out into the open, Ochek reached up and grabbed his beak, holding it shut so that Tahtakiw couldn't alert the man to their presence.

"Quickly!" Ochek whispered.

Morgan put the knot over Tahtakiw's beak and pulled, forcing it to stay shut. Ochek yanked the crane out of the window. Once in the air, Tahtakiw kept flying, away from the island and out across the water, pulling at the string with his feather-fingers on the way in an attempt to get the slipknot off.

With Tahtakiw gone, Morgan locked her fingers together to boost Ochek up. Once he was on the window-sill, she signaled to Arik, who ran to the canoe and jumped inside. Both she and Eli were ready for a clean getaway.

Morgan turned back to the window to watch Ochek, who had lowered himself carefully inside and tiptoed across the floor. The man was sleeping in a chair, turned away from Ochek and her, his bald head slumped to one side, snoring loudly with every inhalation. The bag, which looked very much like a burlap sack, hung from the ceiling like a chandelier, with a million tiny shafts of light shooting from it.

To reach the bag, Ochek needed to stand on the foot of the man's bed. He slid his knife out from his belt and began to saw at the twine in agonizingly slow lashes. To keep his balance, because each sawing motion threw him off, he shifted his feet. And each time he shifted his feet, the bed creaked. Over the man's snoring, the creaks weren't all that loud, but Morgan found herself gripping the windowsill so tightly that her knuckles were white. When the job was almost done, Ochek's foot slipped and he stumbled, and the creaks that followed, one after the other, were like thunder.

The man's head jerked to attention.

Ochek flipped the knife around in his paw, ready for an attack, and stood as still as a statue.

Morgan didn't breathe. She lowered her body so that she could only just barely see over the sill.

The man looked as though he was about to turn his head. He would have seen Ochek, and the bag of summer birds hanging perilously from the ceiling. But he just repositioned his head against the back of the chair, still facing away, and the snoring continued.

Ochek looked at Morgan, relieved, and continued his work until there was one last thread holding the bag in place, no thicker than a piece of dental floss. The animal being put his paw underneath the bag, made one last stroke, and it fell silently into his possession.

As soon as Morgan was sure he had the bag of summer birds, she ran to the canoe, and all three of them waited for Ochek. He emerged from the window with the sack over his shoulder and rushed towards them. The sun had fallen by then, and Ochek, with the shining bag in his arms, looked like a miniature sun sprinting out of the darkness, as though eager for the night to end.

The canoe took off from the shore.

Eli, in the bow seat, and Arik, in the stern, powered their paddles through the water, urging the vessel away from the island and ever closer to the land.

"We did it!" Arik cried. "And Tahtakiw is probably still trying to get the knot off his beak!"

"We've *almost* done it," Ochek said, tempering their excitement. He was sitting in the center of the canoe with Morgan, the bag wrapped securely in his arms. "We've a journey still ahead."

"Can't you just let them out of the bag now?" Morgan asked, staring at the bag.

The birds were flying around inside like they'd chugged coffee, bumping against the fabric like little heartbeats. She heard muffled, excited chirping.

"Not yet," Ochek said. "We need to ensure the Green Time begins in Misewa, for the sake of the others."

"The closer the better," Arik said.

"Paddle faster and stop talking if you want to be closer!" said Eli, who'd been doing most of the work.

Morgan looked back at the squirrel, who picked up the pace after Eli's command.

Their moment of success, a moment that couldn't have seemed more distant when they'd left Misewa, then demanded silence. Calm. There was a gentle and cool breeze. The moon and its white light glowing overhead. Morgan spread her fingers out, touched her fingertips to the water, and watched the trails left behind. The four lines continued to spread farther apart behind the boat, like tiny wakes.

Thwap.

Ochek hunched over, and the bag fell from his arms.

"Ochek!" Morgan lunged towards him, lifted his head.

He was grimacing in pain, clutching his shoulder. Morgan moved his paw to find an arrowhead sticking out from beneath his fur. She looked behind him, on the other side of his shoulder, to find the end of the arrow protruding from his body, its beautiful, terrible feathers illuminated by the bag of summer birds.

Whooosh.

Another arrow zipped past Morgan's head. She looked towards the island to see the man on the shore, aiming his bow towards the canoe.

TWENTY-TWO

"Get down!" Morgan shouted.

While the other two ducked as low as they could, Morgan eased Ochek onto his side. She lay down beside him. He had his paw on the wound, and she had her hand over it, applying pressure, trying to stem the flow of blood, which was bubbling up around the shaft of the arrow. Eli started to sit up, so that he could paddle the canoe to shore, but Arik shouted at him from the stern.

"You'll do nothing of the sort, little one! I've got this!"

"I'm bigger than you!" Eli said.

"Yes, well . . ." Arik sat up, grabbed the paddle she'd dropped in the initial panic, and started paddling. "I have seniority."

Eli relented and stayed down.

Arik was trying to stay low while paddling the canoe towards the eastern shore, but she was still the most exposed of any of them. More than that, the bag holding the summer birds burned bright and made them an easy target.

Sitting ducks, as Arik had said earlier.

Another arrow narrowly missed them, striking the side of the canoe with a heavy thud. The man was still at the shore, firing arrows towards them. The farther they went, however, the less accurate he was.

"At least paddle faster than I would have!" Eli said.

"Everybody's a critic!" Arik said.

"What can I do?" Morgan asked Ochek, her hand caked with blood.

"Nothing," Ochek grunted. "Not until we get to safety."

Thwack.

An arrow hit the stern seat, narrowly missing Arik; an inch higher and it would have hit Morgan's leg.

Splish.

Another disappeared into the lake behind them.

They were out of range.

When the arrows started hitting the water behind them consistently, shot after shot, Eli joined in on the paddling while Morgan sat up and rested Ochek's head on her lap.

As the canoe came to the shore, they heard the man call out from across the lake, "You'll pay for this!"

Arik broke off the end of the arrow in Ochek's shoulder, leaving the rest of it in his body until they could properly treat it. She ripped his shirt in several pieces, then stuffed fabric against the wound at the front and the back and tied it down with a longer strip.

"Can you walk?" she asked him.

He nodded. "I think so."

"And, you know, if you find you're able to run, do that," she said.

They retrieved their packs and off they went through the forest, Arik supporting Ochek, his arm around her shoulders and her arm around his waist. The bag of summer birds was now entrusted with Morgan. She ran with it cradled in her arms and found it hard to look at anything else, the countless shafts of light bombarding her with warmth. Beating rapidly from the birds' frenetic movement. And weightless, like carrying air. How could something that kept an entire world alive be that way? She knew that birds were light, but it seemed a miracle to her.

"Can anybody see the man?" Arik asked while the island was still in view.

"No!" Eli was trailing behind the group, keeping watch.

"Can he swim?" Morgan asked.

"I guess we'll find out, won't we?" Arik said. "Either way, we have a head start."

After the forest came the mountain, and their run slowed to a walk. Still, Ochek refused to stop. And though the journey was difficult, it was made easier by the summer birds; their heat, even from inside the bag, was melting the remaining snow and ice as they went, almost instantly. The Green Time was like a wave rolling to the shore, cascading across the landscape as fast as the four of them could go.

They reached the summit deep into the night, and the man was nowhere to be seen. They hurried across it, through the grove, and found the hut still there.

Abandoned.

Mahihkan was nowhere to be found. The only trace of the great beast was his blood against the surface of the hut, and bandages that he'd torn off his wounds. With their worries about the man, this wasn't something any of them gave much thought to, except that Morgan did lift the bag above her head to light the grove and see if the wolf was hiding in the shadows or collapsed somewhere in the trees.

Ochek was placed where the wolf had been. Eli started a fire like his life depended on it. Arik took the fabric away from Ochek's wound. Blood continued to stream from it. If it were at all possible for an animal to look pale, even though covered in fur, Ochek did. His mouth was dry, his black eyes sunken, almost gray.

Arik pulled a log out of the fire and handed it to Morgan.

"What am I supposed to do with this?" Morgan asked.

"Hold it over the wound," Arik said. "When I pull out the arrow, push it against his skin."

"What? No!"

"Iskwésis, please. He needs us."

"Alright, fine."

"Eli, hold him down."

Eli pushed down on both of Ochek's shoulders as hard as he could.

"On three," Arik said. "One . . . two . . . three!"

Arik pulled the arrow out of Ochek's shoulder, and immediately Morgan thrust the burning wood onto the wound and held it there. Ochek's back arched and he screamed. Morgan pulled the wood away, and she and Arik inspected the area. It had been cauterized.

Morgan fell back against the side of the hut, threw the wood into the fire, and covered her face, sobbing uncontrollably. Arik covered Ochek's wound with a strip of hide and kept her paw there. She tried to comfort the animal being. Eli did the same for Morgan. He knelt beside her, put his arms around her, and she just fell into the embrace.

Seconds turned to minutes, and time continued to pass, until the shock of it all began to fade. Morgan and Eli let go of each other. Arik sat at Ochek's side, dabbing his head and his wounds with a damp cloth.

"We did it, oh crotchety one," Arik said.

Ochek strained to sit and talk. "You'd be . . . grumpy too, if you'd been . . . shot . . . with an arrow."

"Oh my dear Creator," Arik said, breathless.

"What is it?" Eli asked.

"Something's not right," she said.

"What's wrong? What happened?" Morgan asked.

"Ochek is still funny," Arik said. "I thought I'd pulled out his funny along with the arrow."

Morgan slapped Arik on the arm. "You jerk, you scared us!"

Ochek put a paw on her hand, and their eyes met. "It'll be . . . okay . . ."

"I . . ." But more tears came from Morgan's eyes than words from her mouth.

"I could get used to this kinder, gentler Ochek, though," Arik said. "I suppose when an entire village relies on you for food, there isn't much room for comedy, is there? Good news: all that's about to change. We should rest until the morning and then head out to—"

A whipping sound came from outside the hut just before an arrow ripped through the hide and missed Arik by an inch before exiting out the back of the structure as fast as it had entered.

"He's found us!" Eli shouted.

They got onto their stomachs and lay flat against the ground. All of them, that is, except Ochek. He forced himself to his feet with the bag of summer birds grasped firmly in his paw, and made for the flap.

"What are you doing?" Arik asked.

"Ochek, no!" Eli shouted.

"No . . . time . . . to bring . . . the birds . . . to Misewa . . . now." Ochek pushed the flap open.

He left the hut and disappeared from view as another arrow narrowly missed him and all the others. Morgan got to her feet first, followed by the other two, and they ran out of the hut to find Ochek climbing the sequoia.

"What the heck does he think he's doing?" Morgan ran to the tree, intending to pull Ochek down, but he was already out of reach.

"He's letting the birds go as high as he can," Eli said. "So they can get to Misewa."

"And not get captured by the man again," Arik said.

"No! Ochek! No! You can't do this!" Morgan grabbed onto a branch and began to pull herself up, to chase after him, when another arrow came from the darkness within the grove and stuck into the tree right by her head. *Thump*. She let go and tumbled to the ground.

Ochek stopped for a moment and looked down at Morgan. Their eyes met.

"You saved my life," Morgan cried.

Ochek looked at her for one second longer. "And you saved mine, Morgan."

He began to climb again, faster and higher, and soon he

was so far up, so close to the sky, that all you could see was the bag of summer birds and its generous light.

Another arrow came and stuck into a branch right in front of Ochek's head. He didn't stop climbing. Higher and higher still. Higher, until he was above everything: the land to the west, where the cabin lay, where the Green Time had been for so many years, and the land to the east, where Misewa was. Below him, the world was already changing. The snow was melting away. The trees were starting to bud. The cold air was pushed out by the warmth.

Ochek started to open the bag. The birds began to shine brighter, burn hotter. He was straddling the tree at the very top of it.

"No!" the man shouted. He raised his bow.

Morgan didn't think. She got up from the ground and charged at the man. "Stop! Don't do—"

Thwip.

The arrow was released. Morgan slid to a stop and fell to her knees, following the arching projectile with her eyes.

Far above, the orb of light at the tip of the sequoia burst open, and a shock wave of light pulsed across the land just as the arrow connected with its target. Ochek plummeted towards Askí as seven ribbons of light streaked away from the tree, to the east, towards Misewa.

TWENTY-THREE

A rik sped towards the base of the tree, her arms outstretched, ready to try to catch Ochek. He was falling
too fast, though, and just before he collided with the
ground, Arik, like Morgan, crumpled to her knees.

But Ochek never did hit the earth.

Mere feet away, he stopped, suspended in midair. His
paws were in front of his body to break the fall. His legs
were sprawled out. His eyes were shut tight. There was an
arrow through his tail, the weapon that had caused his fall.
Ochek's tail was broken and limp.

Morgan walked back to the tree, got onto her hands and
knees, and looked underneath Ochek. There was nothing to
see. Nothing between him and the ground but air. Eli got
down to look too. The siblings were followed by Arik, who
waved her paws across the open space.

"I don't understand this," Arik said.

"I don't either," Eli said.

"Look!" Morgan gasped.

Something began to form in the space between Ochek and the ground. It started as a small, glowing mass no bigger than the size of a golf ball. Baby-blue and pink. Flashes of light crackled from within the object like lightning. Then it imploded, and a small eruption gave way to a cloud with the same colors, with the same flashes of light. The cloud expanded until it filled the space underneath Ochek's body.

Gradually, eight tendrils grew out of the cloud, and two shorter ones on either side of it. Hands. The tendrils curled up protectively, cupping Ochek within their grasp, then lifted him away from the ground and towards the sky. Up, higher and higher, alongside the sequoia and above it, higher and higher, closer and closer to the sky. Everyone on the summit watched in awe, startled by the beauty. Even the man didn't move.

The farther away Ochek got from the land, the closer to the sky, the brighter the stars burned, as though to welcome him.

For the first time, Morgan remembered more of her home than just the word her mother had said, more than just the room they'd been in, more than just a pull. She remembered the quiet of it and how the quiet brought calm. How, even as a toddler, standing on the steps in front of her house, the calm gave her time to notice the little things. A country sky and the stars speckled across its black canvas, impossibly close and infinite and beautiful.

Suddenly and magnificently, Ochek erupted like fireworks. Seven stars spread apart, then settled into place.

Four of the stars came to rest in the shape of a square, while the other three trailed away from the square in a jagged line.

"Guys," Arik whispered. "I don't think he's coming back down."

A voice came into Morgan's head.

"Ochek has completed a great task for his fellow beings."

She looked around, worried that she'd gone crazy, but then locked eyes with Arik and Eli and knew they heard it in their heads too.

"Kisémanitou," Arik said.

"Creator," Eli whispered.

"In the process, he has sacrificed his own life. For that, he will be honored."

Morgan wiped tears away from her cheeks, but they kept coming, and she gave up trying to stop them.

Creator continued, *"From now on, he will be known as Ochekatchakosuk. He will be in the sky forever, to remind all of the beings living on Aski of what lay in the past, the gift they have been given now, and what could happen again if the land, and all it has to lend, is not respected."*

As quickly as it came, the voice of Creator was gone, and the summit fell deadly quiet.

Morgan, Arik, and Eli were left marveling at the new constellation in the night sky. The snow had melted away. The Green Time had returned. Their journey was complete. They didn't notice, but they were all holding hands as they stood, like a line of paper dolls.

"The land is mine!" The man's ugly, booming voice broke the silence.

Morgan turned towards him. She felt hot all through her body. Her heart was pounding. *Thump. Thump. Thump.* "Yours?! You lost! Nothing is yours! The land belongs to nobody! You suck!"

"You watch your mouth, kid!" the man shouted.

"Hey!" Eli stepped in front of Morgan. "Don't talk to my sister like that!"

The man wasn't intimidated by Eli, despite the boy's best efforts. He moved closer towards the siblings, and Morgan got a good look at him for the first time. He had ragged blue overalls that looked like work pants of some kind, and over those he wore a leather vest that looked as clumsily made as the rack outside his cabin. A quiver full of arrows was strapped to his back. He had blue eyes that looked tired and empty, a scraggly, dirty-blond beard with flecks of gray, and his head was bald, as she'd noticed earlier in his cabin.

He was just an ordinary, middle-aged white man.

"You took everything from me." The man raised his bow and reached behind his back to find another arrow.

"Um, children," Arik whispered, "I appreciate your bravado, but maybe it's time to go."

"Maybe you're right," Morgan said.

As the man pulled an arrow out of his quiver, the trio took off before he could arm the weapon and shoot. They ran through the grove, under the cover of trees. Morgan heard an arrow strike wood just as they came to the mountainside. They didn't break stride.

He was coming.

TWENTY-FOUR

The Green Time had swept across the land, affecting the trees, the air, and the ground underfoot. The path that had been only suggested before was clear now. Arik, Morgan, and Eli followed the path when it went straight and ignored it when it veered off. The man was bearing down on them. Morgan could hear his footsteps.

As he tracked them, he shouted out threats, which felt sharper than arrows, and more deadly.

"I'll kill you!"

"I'm going to eat you for supper!"

"You can't run forever!"

They may not have been able to run forever, but his threats did make the group run faster. They crashed through groves and jumped off short cliff faces that populated the mountainside, never letting up.

The canyon drew closer—and the bridge that would lead them to Misewa. When an arrow whizzed by their heads or hit a tree close by with a sharp *thwack!*, they didn't look.

They kept running. If the man stopped to shoot, it meant they had the slightest bit more space between them and him. There was no time to talk, no time to slow up.

"To the bridge, children!" Arik shouted when they came to the base of the mountain.

They sprinted towards the canyon. Morgan turned around to see the man. He was running after them, no more than fifty yards off.

"Hurry!" Morgan turned back around to find Arik and Eli just standing there, each looking hopeless and defeated. Each staring down at the canyon. "What are you doing?! He's coming!"

"It's gone," Eli said.

"What's gone, what . . . ?" But Morgan saw what Eli meant. The ice bridge had melted away, the new warmth leaving only a portion of it behind, an icicle protruding from the other side.

Too far away from them.

Too far to jump.

Too far to help them across.

"We need to get to the wood bridge," Arik said.

But there was no time, and they all knew it. The man had caught up to them while they stared into the abyss. He was standing twenty feet away, his bow in one hand at the ready, an arrow in the other.

"I had the good life over the mountains!" The man was panting from the chase. "You all took it away from me!"

He raised his bow and aimed the arrow directly at Morgan.

"*That* is not the good life." Arik stepped in front of Morgan. "You're mistaken."

"Move, squirrel!" the man said.

"My name is Arikwachas," she said. "And you suck!" She turned around to Morgan and whispered, "Did I use that right?"

"Yeah, that was pretty good," Morgan whispered back.

"I don't care what your name is! Move!" the man said.

"It's Arik for short, but you can't call me that because my friends call me that."

"Are you trying to *not* get shot?" the man asked.

"Okay"—she hesitated—"you can call me Arik."

"I'm still going to shoot you," the man said.

Arik turned to the children. "Well, that didn't work."

"What were you going for there?" Morgan asked.

Arik shrugged.

Morgan put her hand on Arik's shoulder and moved her aside. She walked forward a few steps, and stopped. Morgan focused on the arrowhead at first, which was aimed directly at her chest, her rapidly beating heart. Then she looked the man right in the eyes. *Stay calm*, she thought. *Stay calm*. She pushed the burning feeling deep down and kept her voice steady.

"What's *your* name?"

The man lowered the bow, then aimed it again at Morgan. "Mason. I guess you might as well know my name before I kill you."

"They call me Iskwésis here," she said. "It means 'Girl'."

"Good for you! Again, I don't care!"

"Calm down. We're just talking."

"I'm done talking. This isn't a movie where you can just stall until you get rescued. Nobody is coming to save you."

216

Arik stood beside Morgan. "You were given as much as you needed, but you decided to take even more. We could have all lived together. We *were* living together."

"Well, *Arik*, what you were giving me wasn't enough."

Mason's eyes looked wild. That's when Morgan saw it. His body, like those of the animals she'd seen in Misewa, looked thin. Emaciated. His clothing, like Ochek's, looked too big for him. He had moved away with the Green Time but was starving all the same.

"You're always going to starve, no matter where you go, no matter how much is there for you," she said.

"Shut up!" Mason said. "Are you trying to guilt me? I'm going to take all three of you back and cook you!"

"Oh, so you were actually serious about that?" Arik asked. "You weren't just mad?"

"Of course I was serious!" the man said.

"Gross," Arik mumbled.

"What's your problem?" Morgan asked. "The Green Time is for everybody. So are all the other seasons. If you don't like the winter, too bad; it's, like, a couple of months. *They've* lived through it for years in a row! Just deal with it!"

"If I can have five months of warmth, why can't I have twelve months of warmth?" Mason asked.

"Because you don't deserve it. Can't you hear yourself talking?"

"Who are you to say what I deserve? What do *you* deserve?"

Morgan tried to hide the fact that her whole body was shaking. She tried not to feel her heart thumping. She looked away from the arrow and locked eyes with Arik, and then, finally, Eli. "I just want to be with my family."

Arik stepped in front of Morgan. "You'll have to kill me to get to her."

"And me." Eli stepped in front of Arik.

"Don't be silly. Get behind me," Arik whispered to Eli, then she shuffled in front of him. "Honestly, if anybody's going to get shot, it'll be the squirrel that's been alive for hundreds of years."

"Why do you kids even care about this place?" Mason asked. "Who do you think you are?"

"I know exactly who I am," Morgan said. "Do you? How did you even get here?"

How *did* he get here? Morgan didn't think he would answer, but it was a mystery she wanted to solve. If he'd come through the Great Tree, then wouldn't he have come through Katie and James's house? Was he some random guy who'd found something while breaking and entering? Was it by chance alone?

"You know what? That's enough," Mason said.

Morgan heard the bowstring tighten as he pulled it back to touch his chin. She could see everything so clearly under the white moon, under the brilliant stars. She took Eli's hand and held it tight, and focused on the stars, on the new constellation that had been made. *Ochekatchakosuk.* She focused on the constellation, then closed her eyes.

She expected to feel an arrow enter her body, but instead she heard a roar that echoed across the North Country. She opened her eyes and looked in the direction the roar had come from. A pair of bright-yellow eyes descended from the mountain and approached the canyon, accompanied by a low and continuous growl that made the ground tremble.

"Good." Mason lowered his bow and arrow. "I was wondering where you were. I won't have to waste more arrows. Kill them."

"No! We saved you!" Eli said.

"Once they're out of the way," Mason said, "we'll find the summer birds and bring them back to where they belong."

"They don't belong to anybody," Arik said. "They are creatures of Kisémanitou. You know this, Mahihkan."

"I said kill them!" Mason shouted.

Mahihkan looked back and forth, from Mason to the humans and Arik, then he howled towards the sky in agony.

"Now!" Mason shouted again.

The wolf took a step towards the travelers, but stopped.

"Fine, you stupid dog!" Mason raised his bow for a final time, pulled back the string, and aimed the arrow at Morgan. "I'll do it myself."

Mahihkan let out an ear-shattering roar and leaped towards the man, knocking him over as he released the string. The arrow careened towards the canyon, far from Morgan. The wolf and Mason rolled violently across the ground and towards the canyon's edge before disappearing over the side.

The siblings rushed to where man and wolf had fallen off. Mahihkan was grasping at the edge with one paw. Mason had fallen all the way down to the bottom, disappearing into the thawed river so far below. Eli wrapped his hands around the wolf's front leg and gripped it tightly. Morgan reached down and took hold as well.

But he was so heavy.

"Get your other leg up!" Morgan said.

Mahihkan tried but couldn't get a hold. His leg was slipping out of their grasp. Arik leaned over and grabbed hold too, so all three of them were trying to keep the wolf from falling, but Mahihkan's leg kept sliding away.

"Try again!" Eli said.

But this time, Mahihkan didn't try. He looked up with his piercing yellow eyes, and his paw slipped. Morgan looked for as long as she dared, then turned away before he hit the water.

All she heard was the splash.

TWENTY-FIVE

Morgan, Eli, and Arik stood at the edge of the canyon and stared out over the North Country. It was surreal, looking at it now, with the sun just beginning to crest above the horizon and painting the earthly colors of Askí with warmth. It looked as though the White Time had never been there at all, but of course, that wasn't the case. Too much had happened. Too many lives had been lost over the years since the White Time began its unrelenting stay, and too many had been lost just in the last week. They were all crying, in their own way and for their own reasons. At the hope the Green Time brought. At the loss of a great hunter who'd long provided for his village and had made the ultimate sacrifice for them. At the loss of an enemy, who, in his last moments, had become an ally.

Morgan took her brother's hand.

"You okay?" she asked.

"Yeah," he said. "It's just . . ."

"Tell me." She nudged him. "I'm your sister, you know. We've got to tell each other things, right?"

"He tried to kill me," he said. "Then he saved us."

"I know he did," she said. "He changed."

Eli looked towards the sky. Ochek wasn't visible any longer, but he was there. Morgan could feel it, and she knew that Eli could too.

"It's not fair that Mahihkan just died, and that's all," Eli said.

"You don't know that," Morgan said. "Not really."

"Whenever anybody here looks up at the sky, they'll know what Ochek did, but they won't know about Mahihkan."

"That's not true," Arik said. "His story will be told through Ochek, and all of us. We will remember the great hunter, and we will remember the wolf, the children, and maybe even the squirrel . . . the jury's out on that one." She cleared her throat awkwardly. "The point being, they will be honored. Plus, who wants to be in the sky forever, just turning around and around and with a broken tail, no less? Boring."

"Arik, you really could've stopped at the whole 'they will be honored' part." Morgan placed both hands on Eli's shoulders. "Arik's right, though. Not about the boring part, but the other thing. They'll all be remembered."

Eli nodded quickly. "Okay."

"And what's most important is that *you'll* remember. Nobody's really gone if they aren't forgotten," Morgan said. "Draw a picture of him."

"Maybe don't remember the part where he wanted to eat you, though," Arik said. "Just, you know, all the after-wanting-to-eat-you things."

Morgan rolled her eyes at Arik but laughed at the same time, and so did Eli. She tugged at Eli's hand. "Come on. Let's go home."

It had been seven days since she'd arrived in the North Country and crossed the Barren Grounds. By the time they crossed through the portal, it would be just in time for breakfast.

They walked along the canyon to find a place they could cross, and if it wasn't before the tree bridge, then it wouldn't be until then. They were hungry, but okay, and there was no urgency now, just a pang in their stomachs. The North Country had been saved, the Green Time was back, and they'd find something to eat on the way to Misewa if they were lucky.

Several hours into their walk along the canyon, they came to the end of the mountain range and the beginning of the forest, where the canyon cut through, eventually leading to the tree bridge. But there was no point in walking hours more when there were perfectly good tree bridges all around them, just waiting to be of service. So they found a tree that grew near the canyon and appeared long enough to stretch across to the other side. They'd brought Ochek's hatchet with them, and they set to work on chopping the tree down. It was hard work with such a small tool, and they took turns at the job. Of course, they didn't need to stop for lunch because they had nothing to eat. By midday, they'd cut a large enough section out of the east side of the tree, and they gathered on the west side to push it down in the proper direction. If it fell the wrong way, it would end up at the bottom of the canyon, and at that point, they may as well walk the rest of the way to the already-felled tree.

They pushed with all their strength. The tree cracked and creaked as it started its descent. The trio stepped back and watched with bated breath. When the top of the tree slammed against the ground on the other side of the canyon, then stayed there after settling, they jumped and cheered and hugged. For that moment, each one of them was able to forget the losses they'd experienced and feel nothing but joy that they were even closer to home.

Arik went first, bouncing over the newly made tree bridge with grace, even the last part of it, which was more difficult because of the branches with their fresh leaves.

"Do you want me to go first?" Eli asked.

Morgan took a deep breath and let it out slowly. "No. I'll go."

She climbed up onto the tree where it had broken off from the ground, stuck both her arms out for balance, and made her way across. She looked straight ahead, keeping her eyes on Arik, who was sitting on the edge of the canyon cheering her on.

"One step at a time," she said to herself, and she repeated that same phrase until she came to the branches.

She stepped around them carefully, holding on to them for balance, and when she made it to the other side, she jumped off triumphantly, landing solidly on two feet. Arik got up and gave her a hug, and Morgan tried to give the squirrel a high five, but Arik had never done a high five before, so it all turned out very awkward. But they were happy nonetheless.

After Eli joined them, they continued on their way towards Misewa with no more obstacles in their way, other than the anticipation of getting there and hunger from not having eaten for so long.

But even that changed for the better.

With the snow gone and the trees full and the weather warm and the waters thawed, four-legged animals and birds and fish had returned to the area. The group first noticed this when walking by a stream, where Arik saw a fish gliding through the water. While she noticed it too late to catch it, it gave them hope. Next, it was a bird soaring through the sky far above them, and another landing on a branch overhead.

Soon after, Eli put a hand on Morgan and another on Arik to stop them.

"Shhh." He pointed through the trees, where, to the right of them, was a rabbit.

"Wapos!" Arik whispered, but in such a way that it sounded like she wanted to shout.

She was almost too loud. The rabbit, which had been sitting there oblivious, perked its ears up. They stood still, as though the White Time had never left and they were all ice statues.

When the rabbit relaxed again and started nibbling on some grass, Morgan asked, "What do we do?"

"I think this is where I come in." Arik took off like a rocket.

As Morgan watched, she couldn't help but think of the first time she and Eli had met the squirrel, how fast she'd run away from Ochek. She looked even faster now, and the rabbit didn't get far before she caught it and wrestled it to the ground. Moments later, it was dead. Before Arik brought the animal back to them, she said a prayer over it, thanking Creator for its sacrifice.

"I bet that's something Mason never did," Morgan said.

"Maybe he didn't kill all the animals over the mountain," Eli said. "He didn't honor their sacrifice, so Creator took them away."

"Or he did, but over here, they were just looking for food, like Ochek and Arik," Morgan guessed. "There was nothing to eat here, so they went somewhere else."

"I just hope they come back all over the North Country," he said.

"Me too."

They ate their meal right there. Eli prepared the fire, work that he'd become quite good at under Ochek's tutelage, and Arik showed Morgan how to prepare the meat. They skinned the rabbit and cooked it over the fire on a spit of Morgan's making, and when it was ready, they all ate their share. The meat was soft and fresh, and each one of them agreed that it was the best food any of them had ever had. By the time they'd packed up, more game had flooded into the area.

Full of food, the three of them moved faster, stopping only so that Arik could catch another rabbit and a prairie chicken to bring back for the villagers. Soon, the sun dipped below the horizon and night fell over the North Country, but they kept walking because they were too excited to camp for the night. They felt even more motivated when the stars began to shine overhead and they saw Ochek looking down on them with his square body and broken tail.

"It's like he's following us," Morgan said.

Ochek did look that way. His constellation was bright and clear through the trees, and always directly over them, watching protectively.

"I think he's doing exactly that," Arik agreed.

After they'd hiked for a while longer, they saw lights flickering in the distance. They looked like fireflies. As they got closer, they saw that the lights weren't fireflies at all, but a series of torches, all in a line. It was the villagers of Misewa, standing in a circle in the clearing in front of the Council Hut, each one of them carrying a torch, waiting to welcome the travelers home. Muskwa was in the middle of the circle, standing tall and proud and looking younger than when they'd seen him the first time.

Morgan, Eli, and Arik walked into the circle, where they met the great bear.

Arik took the game she'd caught off her shoulders and placed it at Muskwa's feet. Muskwa nodded towards one of the foxes, and they gathered the food up and took it away.

"You've done a good thing, Arikwachas," Muskwa said.

"Ekosani, Muskwa," Arik said. "And you can call me Arik, if you like, Chief."

"Dear Arik," Muskwa said, "would you like this to be your home?"

"Muskwa . . ." Arik sounded breathless, unable to find the words for once.

"And not only because it'll protect our traps." Muskwa chuckled.

"Ehe, Chief Muskwa," Arik said. "I would be proud to live here."

"Good." Muskwa took a long, sad look at the sky, at the Ochek constellation, which had followed the travelers all the way there. "You may stay in Ochek's lodge."

Arik nodded, then backed away to beside the humans.

"Children," Muskwa said. "Come forward."

Eli and Morgan did as asked.

"How do you know about Ochek?" Morgan asked.

"Only speak when spoken to!" Eli said to his sister.

"It's okay, young one," Muskwa said. "We saw the explosion of light, from here in Misewa, and the new stars in the sky. The Green Time danced through our village in a heavy, warm wind." Muskwa closed his eyes, as though to pray. "Then Kisémanitou spoke to all of us, about what had happened. About our great hunter's sacrifice."

The bear opened his eyes and looked at the two children, nodding his head.

"You've done a selfless thing for this village," Muskwa said. "We honor you for that. You could have left, but you chose to stay and help us. Help Ochek." He offered each sibling a tobacco tie, placing the sacred medicine in their left hands.

"It wasn't us," Morgan said. "It was Ochek. We didn't even—"

"And Mahihkan too," Eli added.

Muskwa looked the travelers over, from Arik to Eli to Morgan. "Each one of you had a role, big or small, in bringing the Green Time back to the North Country. This story will be passed down from one generation to the next. We will not forget what has happened here."

"I don't think we'll ever forget it either," Morgan said.

"You're welcome to stay longer, if you wish," Muskwa said.

"Can we?" Eli asked Morgan.

Morgan shook her head. She answered to Muskwa, but kept her eyes on Eli. "Thanks for the offer, but we can't. There are people waiting for us back home."

Eli's lips began to quiver, his eyes began to water, but he nodded reluctantly.

"We can come back," she said to Eli. "If that's okay with you," she said to Muskwa.

"You will always be welcome here," Muskwa said. "And you're welcome, too, to stay till morning, rather than travel across the Barren Grounds at night."

"That's okay," Morgan said. "I'm not afraid of the dark."

TWENTY-SIX

Morgan and Eli left Misewa behind, their path ahead illuminated by a line of villagers carrying torches and standing at the beginning of the Barren Grounds, where they would send them off. They had their own torches, for when the villagers' lights dimmed, and Arik was with them. The squirrel had insisted on accompanying the kids, not because she was worried for their safety or because she thought that Morgan was actually afraid of the dark, but rather because she found them such good company.

The Barren Grounds weren't as intimidating now that the White Time had ended. It was a flat and uninhabited land that stretched wide from east to west and appeared to lead right into the horizon. Upon careful inspection, Morgan could see the mountains to the far west, and it made her replay the last days of their journey in her mind. She tried to find the sequoia, a landmark for those memories, but wasn't able to. Ahead, she could see the northern woods, like a thin strip of green Velcro holding the sky and the land together.

"What's to the east?" Morgan asked.

She could see nothing in that direction. It was as though the Barren Grounds kept going, right through, until hitting the sky.

"Askí," Arik answered simply.

"Yeah, but . . ."

"What if we were walking through a field where you live and I asked you what lands were to the east?" Arik asked.

"Ontario, I guess," Morgan said.

"And is that all?" Arik asked.

"No, the whole world's after that, until you come right back to Winnipeg."

"Well," Arik said, "the whole of Askí is to the east. There are many more lands, and many more beings, before you end up right back where you started. Here, in Misewa."

Morgan tried to imagine just what the rest of Askí was like. What other villages were there, and what other creatures. Had any other humans gone anywhere else on this world? Were they still here? How?

"What are you thinking about, Iskwésis?" Arik asked.

"Nothing," Morgan said. "Just that, now that we have time to breathe, all of this is sinking in. This place, it's real. And now we have to leave, you know?"

"You said that a week here might be an hour or so back on your world, right?" Arik asked.

"Yeah," she said.

"So you could even come back tomorrow night, *your* tomorrow night, and stay here for a month and explore!" Arik could hardly contain herself.

"We're going to, right, Morgan?" Eli asked.

Morgan didn't feel the excitement that the other two had, and she didn't know why. They could come back. By tomorrow night, maybe in fifteen hours, it would just be . . . well, she didn't know the math, but months. Arik would still be here. Misewa. Ironically, maybe by then it would be winter again, but when it was *supposed* to be winter. She didn't know why she felt upset—until she said, "I just don't want to forget what happened."

"Do you remember those pictures across the walls of the Council Hut?" Arik asked.

Morgan did. "Yeah, they were like wall paintings. The way people used to communicate before we had words." She could picture them: simple, dark ocher paintings that formed something completely beautiful.

"Why do you think those pictures are there?"

"They're stories, aren't they?"

Arik nodded. "They tell the story of this place, of Misewa, so that our history is never forgotten."

"A story brought us here, you know. A picture," Eli said.

"Stories always lead people somewhere," Arik said. "To a place, to a memory."

Morgan knew, then, what Arik meant. "I should write about what happened, so that I won't forget it."

Mrs. Edwards popped into her mind. She *did* have a poem due.

"And so that you won't forget yourself." Arik winked at Morgan, put her arm around Morgan's shoulders, and they kept walking. "But, you know, come back too, of course. For new memories, that is."

Sometime in the middle of the night, they came to the Great Tree. Morgan found that the protection she'd placed over the portal was untouched, the boards still hammered securely into the trunk. The hammer was on the ground in front of the tree, once buried under snow but now in plain sight. Beyond the tree lay the northern woods, which, according to Ochek, nobody had been in for many, many years. She imagined a group of animal beings sleeping right where she stood now, and a giant coming out from the forest and taking the soul of the Elder. It made her shudder.

"Have you ever seen Mistapew?" she asked Arik.

Hearing the name, Arik shuffled back a few inches, as though that might protect her if the giant showed up. "I think if I had seen it, I wouldn't be here with you today." And she added, "I'd prefer not to see it ever, if I have a choice in the matter."

"You know, Mistapew is in our world too," Eli said.

"Well, tell it that I said hi," Arik said.

"Seriously?" Morgan asked Eli. "Like, you don't mean a grainy video from a million miles away, right? You mean actual, real live Mistapew?"

"People in my community have seen it," Eli said.

"I thought those were just legends, like my books," Morgan said. "Like, there's really no such thing as a . . . oh, wait . . . are there talking lions here?"

Arik nodded.

"Okay, strike that," she said. "I guess what I mean is, I haven't seen Bigfoot in Katie and James's house the last two months. And there aren't sightings in the city, so how do they get all the way through the city, into the woods, never mind the attic?"

Arik leaned back and looked at the sky thoughtfully. "You think that this portal is the only one? Interesting."

Morgan's head jerked towards Arik. "What? There are more?"

"I mean, anything's possible." Arik peered into the darkness of the thick ancient forest. "Nobody has been in the northern woods for generations, so who's really to say?"

"Ever since the Elder's soul was taken?" Eli asked.

"Ehe," Arik said. "And they never even made it into the woods either. There are no stories of pisiskowak that have."

"Now *that* would be an adventure, wouldn't it?" Morgan asked.

"Be my guest," Arik said. "I'm perfectly happy right here."

"On second thought," Morgan said, "I'm all adventured out."

"Maybe tomorrow night," Eli said.

"Maybe tomorrow night," Morgan echoed.

She picked up the hammer and pried the boards away from the tree. One by one, the boards were placed on the ground, leaning against the trunk of the Great Tree, and, little by little, the attic was revealed.

"That's earth?" Arik asked. "Yuck."

"I mean, that's a room on earth," Morgan said. "There's a little more to it than this."

"Yes, I was just thinking that I thought it would be bigger," Arik said.

Morgan placed the hammer against the tree, alongside the boards. "For next time."

"Won't those construction guys wonder where their hammer is?" Eli asked.

"*Pfft*. They might if they ever actually showed up."

With the portal open, there was only one thing left to do, but nobody really seemed to want to do it. So, for a long while, all three of them just stared at each other. Then, without warning, Arik pulled both Morgan and Eli into an embrace.

"I'll miss you both," she said.

"We'll miss you too," Morgan said.

"I won't see you for months, but you'll see me tomorrow," Arik said.

"It'll feel like months," Eli said.

"I *am* very miss-able," Arik said, "but I'm certain you'll survive."

She helped Morgan and Eli through the portal, back into the attic.

The attic had dried out. And there was no reason to worry that the cold would creep into their foster parents' bedroom. It was probably warmer in the attic than it was outside. Outside in Winnipeg, maybe not in the North Country.

"But why is it all dried out?" Morgan asked out loud. "It's been the Green Time for, what, a day? Wouldn't that only be, like, ten or twenty minutes on earth?" She rubbed her feet against the plywood floor just to make sure she wasn't imagining it, then bent down and touched it. It was dry as a bone.

"There must be a space around the Great Tree, including your little room, where our times intersect," Arik said. "It's probably why I'm not moving ten thousand miles a minute right now in your eyes."

"That's so weird," Morgan said. It was true though. Arik was on Askí, she and Eli were on earth, but they were all in the same *time*.

"If that's the case," Arik said, "we could just sit here and chat forever if you wanted."

But they really couldn't. Even if the attic was on Misewa time, by the light coming in through the crack between the door and the floor, Morgan could tell the sun was rising. Morning was coming whether it was Misewa or earth time, and that meant Katie and James would be up soon.

"We *will* see you again, right?" Morgan turned back towards Arik.

"Oh, I know you will," she said.

"How?" Eli asked.

"Call it a hunch," she said. "Now, I'd best be off. Misewa might fall apart if I'm away for too long, you know."

Arik blew them each a kiss, then scurried off on all fours. Morgan and Eli watched her go until suddenly she darted out of view. Morgan pinched the corner of the drawing.

"Do you want to, or . . . ?"

"No," Eli said. "You can."

Morgan nodded and pulled the paper away from the wall. In an instant, Askí was gone.

The two of them inspected the drawing. It was new, just like the last time it had come off the wall. The Barren Grounds were dry and uninhabited, but across them, in the distance, you could see Arik on her way to Misewa. You could see the forest, lush and green and alive. You could see the village. And, finally, you could see a line of lights in front of the collection of longhouses.

All the animal beings with their torches raised, seeing the humans home.

TWENTY-SEVEN

Morgan could hear Eli flop onto his bed. He'd wanted to stay in Askí, she knew that, but the allure of an actual bed must have trumped that desire. At least for now. Truth be told, in the end, Morgan hadn't wanted to leave either, but at the same time, she knew they would go back, and so she enjoyed flopping onto her own bed too. It felt like a luxury, not unlike the time, they'd had pimíhkán early on in their journey, or wapos, rabbit, near the end of it. Sleeping on the ground in their hut was like jerky and broth; sleeping on a bed was like freshly caught wapos.

It was just before six o'clock in the morning, which meant that she didn't have to get up for a little under an hour. James usually woke up at a quarter to seven. Neither she nor Eli had slept last night in the North Country, and any amount of rest would do.

She closed her eyes.

At first, her mind flooded with memories of her time on Askí. The images that came to her, one after the other, were like a lullaby. Even the bad memories—like the wolf drag-ging Eli out of the hut—presented themselves as steps on a journey. A journey that had led them to saving Misewa, and all of Askí. Okay, Ochek had done the main saving, but she and Eli had played their parts as well, and that was some-thing. She had the tobacco tie in her left palm as proof of their involvement. Of their importance.

Eventually, as the blue glow of the early morning rested over Morgan's body, those images, those memories gave way to a rhythm, like the beat of a drum. *Thump. Thump. Thump. Thump. Thump. Thump. Thump.* Morgan's ear was pressed against the pillow, and she realized that it was her heartbeat. Not pounding out of her chest. Not jackhammer-ing from fear. But beating calmly, methodically. She focused on the rhythm, and as she did, another scene played in her mind of its own accord.

Morgan was walking through a field of deep, untouched snow, in the middle of the night. In the middle of nowhere, out on the land, the night was the blackest black. It was all around her, in all directions, except ahead. There, a square of light shone. She was walking towards it. Lifting her knees up over the surface of the snow, stepping forward, over and over again. Each time she pressed her foot into the snow, a crunching sound rang out through the otherwise quiet space. The crunching sound, no matter how fast she tried to walk, was always in time with the rhythm of the drum, with the beat of her heart.

Thump. Thump. Thump. Thump. Thump. Thump. Thump.

As she came closer to the square of light, Morgan became aware that it was a window at the center of a small house.

A bungalow. The house was at the tree line of a wooded area. Soon, the gentle light stretched towards her, over the snow, like a path, and she followed it all the way to the window. She could see a bedroom through the window. There was a lamp on a side table, and a rocking chair. A woman was sitting in the rocking chair and using the chair as intended, rocking back and forth with a child in her arms.

A young girl no older than three.

Morgan reached forward, as though she could touch them from outside the window, standing knee-deep in the snow. Her fingertips pressed against the cold glass, and she was inside the room. The crunching gave way to her actual heartbeat.

Thump. Thump. Thump. Thump. Thump. Thump. Thump.

She was in the middle of the room, facing the rocking chair. Her mother was in the chair. Her mother's arms were empty. Her mother was crying and whispering one word, over and over, to the rhythm of the drum.

"Kiskisitotaso, kiskisitotaso, kiskisitotaso, kiskis—"

"I haven't," Morgan whispered. "I haven't forgotten myself."

Her mother gasped. She'd been looking towards the door, but looked away from it now, looked up, to Morgan. She stood, and Morgan and her mother were face-to-face.

"I did, maybe," Morgan said, "but I've found myself again."

"My girl," her mother whispered, tears streaming down her cheek, curling over her lips. "My girl. Kisakihitan."

"I love you too," Morgan said. She tasted salt water against her tongue.

Her tears mirrored her mother's, as if somehow they were on the same path, if only right now.

Her mother reached towards Morgan, and Morgan did the same. As soon as their fingertips touched, Morgan felt the same pull she'd felt the first time she'd arrived in the North Country. She felt the pull, then she was pulled away, as though in a vehicle going at light speed. She woke up in her bed, her arm outstretched towards the bedroom window, the tobacco tie clutched in her hand.

When Morgan arrived at the breakfast table after taking her time getting ready for the day, she found James, Katie, and Eli were already there. Their plates were in front of them, but untouched. They were waiting for her. James had prepared a meal exactly like the one he'd made yesterday—over a week ago to Morgan, and even longer for Eli—but the food had not been constructed into faces.

"You look tired," Katie said.

"Yeah." Morgan sat down, ready to dig in to her food.

As soon as she sat down, Eli started in on his meal. Morgan couldn't help but notice the look of relief on the faces of Katie and James.

"Were you guys up all night?" James asked. "Eli looks just about as rough."

"We were hanging out," Morgan said, and her eyes met those of a smiling Eli.

"That's awesome you two are getting along," Katie said.

"He's growing on me." Morgan started to eat. Within seconds she was half-finished. She hadn't noticed how hungry she was until she had a plate of bacon, eggs, and hash browns in front of her.

"Breathe, Morgan!" James laughed.

But Eli was shoveling food into his mouth just as quickly. She couldn't help but imagine the animal beings in Misewa right then, how they'd be able to eat a big meal now. Their meat racks would be full, like their bellies. They'd have fat under their fur, not just skin and bones. By now, it had been over an hour since they'd left. That meant Misewa had been without her and Eli for at least a week. She couldn't wait to see how different things would be when they went back. The day was going to pass slowly. It would be agonizing. By the time Katie and James were asleep, it would be almost fifteen hours from now.

Months in Misewa.

"You wore your moccasins," Katie said.

Morgan looked down at her feet, where, in fact, she was still wearing the black moccasins. To Katie, Morgan had only had them for less than a day. But, oh, the places she had traveled in them. Through blizzards, forests, over canyons and mountains, across the Barren Grounds. They looked months old. Thankfully, Katie didn't seem to notice how dirty and worn they were. She was probably just so happy to see Morgan wear them that those little details escaped her.

"I did," Morgan said. "They're great."

Katie looked to be holding back her emotions, seeing Morgan wear her two-month anniversary present. "You can wear those to school too, you know," Katie said, gathering herself. "Even walking *to* school."

"Really?" Morgan glanced at Eli and winked at her brother. "I totally didn't know you could go on long walks in these things."

"Well, school isn't *that* far," James said. "But maybe you could test them out and see how they hold up?"

"Maybe I could," Morgan said, then she and Eli broke into laughter.

EPILOGUE

"Good morning, Ghost," Emily said.

As usual, after Morgan had walked Eli to his locker, Emily was there to meet her while she exchanged her backpack for her first-period binder and textbook.

"Good morning, Houldsy!" Morgan gave Emily a hug.

Emily patted Morgan on the back for the duration of the hug, while also saying, with a very clear tone of confusion, "I didn't really take you for a hugger there, Morg."

The embrace ended. Somehow, even though she was exhausted, Morgan had so much energy that she felt as though she couldn't contain herself. Like she'd had a cup or five of James's coffee. She was almost bouncing in place at the lockers with Emily. A new kind of dance in the crowd of teens.

"Morg. Morgue. That's ironic because I've never felt so alive!" she said playfully.

"What's gotten into you?" Emily laughed, looking at Morgan sideways. "Yesterday I thought you might spontaneously combust."

"Yesterday . . ." Morgan said thoughtfully. She was still forgetting that to everybody else on earth, the night had passed as a night should pass. Emily had last seen Morgan just yesterday. But Morgan had last seen Emily last week. "Right. Yeah. I just had a good night. I'm a changed girl. Everybody can change, you know."

Emily laughed. They closed their lockers and walked together on their way to English.

"Oh, hey, did that drawing pad work out?" Emily asked. "Did 'the kid living with you' like it?"

"My brother," Morgan said.

"Did your brother like it?" Emily asked.

"Yeah," Morgan said. "We both did."

In English class, Morgan sat at her usual seat, right in front of Mrs. Edwards's desk, close enough to read the spine on her teacher's masterpiece. All ten copies of it. Emily had sat beside Morgan, and when the bell rang to start class, she saw Mrs. Edwards do a double take. Morgan could hardly blame her. It was the first time she had sat beside anybody in ELA. In fact, in all her classes, she'd sat beside somebody only if there was absolutely no other choice.

Morgan had a new poem facedown on her desk, and as soon as Mrs. Edwards sat, Morgan reached over and handed the work to her.

Mrs. Edwards accepted it. "Did you find your passion?"

Morgan looked at Emily, who nodded at her with encouragement, then looked back at her teacher. She'd written it before leaving for school, while the trip with Eli to Misewa was still fresh in her mind. She hadn't left herself much wiggle room, but it was one of those magical times when the words just came out. It was like she wasn't even writing them.

"I think I did," Morgan said.

Mrs. Edwards didn't want to wait to read Morgan's poem. She wheeled the television set to the front of the room—something the entire class was overjoyed to see, even cheered for, because it essentially meant no class. *Stranger Than Fiction* (it was always a movie about writing) started playing moments later.

The students watched the movie, Emily watched Morgan, and Morgan watched Mrs. Edwards's eyes move back and forth. At last she placed the poem on her desk and seemed content to wait out the class while the movie played on.

When the bell rang, all the students filed out of the room except Morgan, who was held back by Mrs. Edwards. The teacher didn't say a word to Morgan, just handed her the sheet of paper, nodded, and left.

Alone now, Morgan flipped over the paper to find red lettering across the top of it.

"I knew you could do more, and I hope you know that now. Now do even better. B+."

"B+?" Morgan started to feel the heat in her chest. She took a deep breath, and the burning sensation went away. She got a B+. So what? There was more inspiration to find on the adventures that lay ahead.

On the Barren Grounds

It took sinking under blinding white
To emerge another me
Somebody I forgot I was
Someone I could never see.

It took facing my worst fears
Stepping out into the night
To find that I was brave enough
Before I found the light.

It took me going far away
To feel this close to you
It took dreaming of a memory
To change what I thought I knew.

It took stars within the sky
To guide my way back home
That I'll always know the way
Wherever I might roam.

DAVID A. ROBERTSON is the recipient of the 2021 Freedom to Read Award and the author of numerous books for young readers including *When We Were Alone* (illustrated by Julie Flett), which won the 2017 Governor General's Literary Award and was nominated for the TD Canadian Children's Literature Award. More recently, he and Julie collaborated for a second time on the picture book *On the Trapline*. Dave's most recent book, *The Great Bear*, is the second book in his series for middle-grade readers, The Misewa Saga. The first book in this series is the critically acclaimed *The Barren Grounds*, which received a starred review from *Kirkus*, was an OLA Silver Birch Fiction Award nominee, and was named an honor book in the USBBY-CBC Outstanding International Trade Book category. A sought-after speaker and educator, Dave is a member of Norway House Cree Nation and currently lives in Winnipeg.

For more information, visit his website: www.darobertson.ca and follow him on Twitter: @DaveAlexRoberts